# The Pony Rider Boys
# In The Rockies

Frank Gee Patchin

1st WORLD
LIBRARY
Literary Society

# The Pony Rider Boys in The Rockies

## Frank Gee Patchin

© 1st World Library – Literary Society, 2005
PO Box 2211
Fairfield, IA 52556
www.1stworldlibrary.org
First Edition

LCCN: 2006902695

Softcover ISBN: 1-4218-1828-0
Hardcover ISBN: 1-4218-1728-4
eBook ISBN: 1-4218-1928-7

Purchase *"The Pony Rider Boys in The Rockies"*
as a traditional bound book at:
www.1stWorldLibrary.org/purchase.asp?ISBN=1-4218-1828-0

1st World Library Literary Society is a nonprofit
organization dedicated to promoting literacy by:

- Creating a free internet library accessible from any
  computer worldwide.
- Hosting writing competitions and offering book
  publishing scholarships.

Readers interested in supporting literacy
through sponsorship, donations or
membership please contact:
literacy@1stworldlibrary.org
Check us out at: www.1stworldlibrary.ORG
and start downloading free ebooks today.

*The Pony Rider Boys in The Rockies*
contributed by Tim, Ed & Rodney
in support of
1st World Library Literary Society

# CONTENTS

# CHAPTER I

## THE LOVE OF A HORSE

"Oh, let me get up. Let me ride him for two minutes, Walter."

Walter Perkins brought his pony to a slow stop and glanced down hesitatingly into the pleading blue eyes of the freckle-faced boy at his side.

"Please! I'll only ride him up to the end of the block and back, and I won't go fast, either. Let me show you how I can ride him," urged Tad Butler, with a note of insistence in his voice.

"If I thought you wouldn't fall off -- "

"I fall off?" sniffed Tad, contemptuously. "I'd like to see the pony that could bounce me off his back. Huh! Guess I know how to ride better than that. Say, Chunky, remember the time when the men from Texas had those ponies here - brought them here to sell?"

Chunky - the third boy of the group - nodded vigorously.

"And didn't I ride a broncho that never had had a saddle on his back but once in his life? Say, did I get thrown then?"

"He did that," endorsed Stacy Brown, who, because of his well-rounded cheeks and ample girth, was known familiarly among his companions as "Chunky." "I mean, he didn't. And he rode the pony three times around the baseball field, too. That broncho's back was humped up like a mad cat's all the way around. 'Course Tad can ride. Wish I could ride half as well as he does. You needn't be afraid, Walter."

Thus reassured by Chunky's praise, Walter dropped the bridle rein over the neck of his handsome new pony, and slid slowly to the ground.

"All right, Tad. Jump up! But don't hold him too tightly. He doesn't like it, and, besides, he has been trained to run when you tighten up on the rein, and father would not like it if we were to race him in the village."

"I'll be careful."

Tad Butler needed no second invitation to try out his companion's pony. With the agility of a cowboy, he leaped into the saddle without so much as touching a foot to the stirrup. In another second, with a slight pressure on the rein, he had wheeled the animal sharply on its haunches, and was jogging off up the street at an easy gallop, both boy and pony rising and falling in graceful, rhythmic movements, as if in reality each were a part of the other. Tad seemed born to stirrup and saddle.

Yet, true to his promise, the boy made no effort to increase the speed of his mount. Nor did he go beyoud

Frank Gee Patchin

the corner named. Instead, he circled and came galloping back, one hand resting lightly on the rein, the other swinging easily at his side.

As he neared the two boys, Tad checked his pony, but Walter motioned to him to continue. With a smile of keen appreciation, Tad shook out the reins, and pony and rider swung on down the village street.

The soft breeze bad by now fanned the bright color into the face of Thaddeus Butler, and his deep blue eyes glowed with excitement and pleasure; for, to him, there was no happiness so great as that to be found on the back of a swift-moving pony.

However, this was a pleasure that seldom came to Tad, for his lines had not fallen altogether in pleasant places. The boy was now seventeen, and from his twelfth birthday he had been almost the sole support of his mother. His time, out of school hours, was spent largely in doing odd jobs about the village where his services were in demand, and on Saturday afternoons and nights he delivered goods for a grocery store, for which latter service he earned the - to him - munificent sum of twenty-five cents. But all of this he accepted cheerfully and manfully. Now and then Tad was allowed to drive the grocer's wagon to the station for goods, and at such times his work was a positive recreation. Some day Tad hoped to have a horse of his own. He could imagine no more perfect happiness than this. He had determined, though, that when he did own one, it should be a saddle horse and a speedy one at that. Yet, at the present moment the realization of his ambition seemed indeed far away.

Walter Perkins was the son of a banker. He and Tad

Butler had been born and brought up in the little village of Chillicothe, Missouri, where they still lived, and, despite the difference in their social positions, had been fast friends since they were little fellows.

Chunky was the son of a merchant in a small town in Massachusetts, and had been visiting an uncle in Chillicothe for nearly a year past.

Walter was a delicate boy, and, reared in luxury, as he had been all his life, he had sensed few of the delights of out-door life that were so apparent in the face of his nimble friend, Tad. It was this delicate physical condition that had brought about the gift of the pony. The family physician had advised it in order that the boy might have more out-door air, and on this May morning Walter had brought the pony out to show to his admiring friends.

"Tad's a good rider. Isn't he a beauty?" breathed Chunky, as they watched the progress of boy and horse down the street.

"Who, Tad?" asked Walter, absorbed in the contemplation of his new possession.

"Tad! Pooh! No; the pony, of course. I don't see anything very fetching about Tad, do you? But I should be willing to be as freckled as he is if I could stick on a pony's back the way he does."

"Yes, he does know how to ride," agreed Walter. "And, by the way, father is going to get a horse for Professor Zepplin, my tutor; then we are going off on long rides every day, after my lessons are done. The doctor says it will be good for me. Fine to have a doctor like that, isn't it?"

"Great! Wish I could go along."

"Why don't you?" asked Walter, turning quickly to his companion. "That would be just the idea. What great times we three could have, riding off into the open country! And we could go on exploring expeditions, too, and make believe we were cowboys and - and all that sort of thing."

Chunky shook his head dubiously. "I haven't a pony. But I wish I had. I should like to go so much," replied the boy wistfully.

"Then, why not ask your uncle to get one for you? He will do it, I know," urged Walter brightly, brimming over with his new plan. "Why, I'll ask him myself."

"I did."

"Wouldn't he do it?"

"No. Uncle said I was too young, and that the first thing I would be doing would be to break my neck. If father was here and gave his permission, why, that would be different. Uncle said it would take my mind off my school, besides."

"School? Why, school will not last much longer. It is May, now, and school will be over early in June. That isn't long to wait. You go right home, Chunky, and tell your uncle you must have a pony. Tell him I said so. If he refuses, I'll have my father go ask him. He won't refuse my father anything he asks. My father is a banker and everybodydoes everything he wants them to, because he lends them money," advised Walter wisely.

"My - my uncle doesn't have to borrow money. He's got money of his own," bristled Chunky.

"Yes, that's so. But you go ask him. Tell him about my pony and that we are all going off for a ride every day. Say that Professor Zepplin will be along to take care of us. And say! I'll tell you what," added the boy eagerly.

"Yes?" urged Chunky.

"We will form ourselves into a club. Now, wouldn't that be great?"

"Fine!" glowed Chunky. "But, what kind of a club? They don't have horses in clubs."

"We shall, in this one. That is, we shall be the club, and the ponies will be our club-house. When we are on our ponies' backs we shall be in our club-house. Maybe we can get Ned Rector to join us. He knows how to ride - why, he rides almost as well as Tad."

Chunky nodded thoughtfully.

"What shall we call it? We must have some kind of a name for the club."

"I hadn't thought of that. I'll tell you what," exclaimed Walter, brightening, after a moment's consideration. "We will call ourselves the Rough Riders. That's what we will do, Chunky."

"Yes, but we are not rough riders," protested Chunky.

"We are only beginners; that is, all of us except Tad, and he can't join us - just because he's too poor to have a horse. As for us - humph! We'd be rough riders only when we fell off!"

Walter laughed heartily.

"No," he admitted. "I guess we are not rough riders yet; but we may be some day, after we've learned to ride better. I can't think of any other name, can you?"

"We might call ourselves the Wild Riders," suggested Chunky.

"No, that won't do, either. It's as bad as the other name. Father'd never let me go out at all if we called ourselves the Wild Riders, because he would think it meant we were going to be too much like cowboys. I guess we shall have to think it over some more. But here comes Tad back. Suppose we ask him? He'll know what to call the club."

Tad reigned in alongside of them and pulled the pony up sharply, patting its sleek neck approvingly, still loath to dismount.

"It's great, fellows. Wish I had a pony like him."

"So do I," echoed Chunky.

"Why, you don't have to touch the reins at all. I could ride him without just as well as with them. All you have to do is to press your knee against his side and he will turn, just as if you were pulling on the rein. He's a trained pony, Walter. Did you know that?"

"That's what the man said when father bought him. Jo-Jo can walk on his hind legs, too. But father said I mustn't try to make him do any tricks, for fear I might get hurt."

"Hurt nothing! He wouldn't hurt a baby," objected Tad in the little animal's defence. "I'll show you - I won't hurt him, don't be afraid," he exclaimed leaping to the ground, stripping the rein over the animal's head and holding it at arm's length. "If he knows how to stand up I can make him do it. I've seen them do that in the circus. Let me have your whip."

"I don't know about that," answered Walter doubtfully. "Yes, you may try," he decided finally, extending the whip that he had been idly tapping against his legging. "But don't hit him, will you?"

"Not I," grinned the freckle-faced boy, leading the pony further out into the street. "He doesn't need to be struck."

Tad first coaxed the pony by patting it gently on the side of the head, to which the intelligent animal responded by brushing his cheek softly with its nose.

"See, he knows a thing or two," cried Tad. "Now, watch me!"

Standing off a few feet, the boy tapped the animal gently under the chin with the whip.

"Up, Jo-Jo! Up!" he urged, lifting the whip into the air insistently. At first, Jo-Jo only swished his tail rebelliously, shaking his head until the bit rattled between his teeth.

But Tad persisted, gently yet firrnly urging with voice and whip. Jo-Jo meanwhile pawed the dirt up into a cloud of dust that settled over the boys, finally causing a chorus of sneezes, until Tad felt sure he observed a twinkle of amusement in the eyes of the knowing little animal.

"Up, Jo-Jo!" he commanded almost sternly, bringing the whip sharply against the side of his own leg.

The pony, recognizing the voice of a master, hesitated no longer. Half folding its slender forelegs back, it rose slowly, up and up.

"Walter Perkins and Stacy Brown broke into a cheer. But Tad, never for an instant removing his gaze from Jo-Jo, held up a warning hand, leaned slightly forward and fixed the pony with impelling eyes.

Then Tad backed away slowly. To the amazement of the others, Jo-Jo, balancing himself beautifully on his hind legs, followed his new-found master in short, cautious steps, the animal's head now high in the air, its nostrils dilated, and every nerve strained to the task in hand.

"Beautiful," breathed Walter and Chunky in chorus.

"He's a regular brick," added Chunky.

"How'd you do it, Tad!"

Before replying, the boy lowered the whip to his side, motioning to the pony that his task was done. Jo-Jo dropped quickly on all fours, and, walking up to Tad, rubbed his nose against the lad's cheek again.

"Good boy," soothed Tad, returning the caress, his eyes swimming with happiness.

But as Tad stepped back Jo-Jo insistently followed, alternately pushing his nose against the boy's face and tugging at his shirt.

"He wants to do it again, Tad," cried Chunky, enthusiastically.

The freckle-faced boy grinned knowingly.

"Got any sugar, Walter?" he asked.

Walter thrust a hand into a trousers pocket, bringing up a handful of lumps that were far from being their natural color. But Tad grabbed them, and an instant later Jo-Jo's quivering upper lip had closed greedily over the handful of sweets.

"That's what the little rascal wanted," breathed Tad with a pleased smile. "I could teach that pony to do 'most anything but talk, fellows. I'm not so sure that he couldn't do that in his own way, after a little time. What did you give for him?"

"Father paid the man a hundred and fifty dollars."

Tad uttered a long-drawn whistle; his face sobered. It was more money than he ever had seen at one time in his life. Would he ever have as much as that? The freckle-faced boy doubted it.

"We fellows were talking about getting up a club," spoke up Walter.

"Club? What kind of a club?" asked Tad absently.

"Oh, some sort of a riding club. Chunky is going to ask his uncle to buy him a pony; then we are going out with my tutor on long rides in the country.

Tad eyed them steadily.

"Somehow we can't just decide on the name for the new club. I thought maybe we would call ourselves the Bough Riders. Chunky doesn't like that name. We had an idea that, perhaps, you could give us one. What do you say, Tad?"

"Chunky's uncle is going to get him a pony?" asked Tad a bit unsteadily.

"We hope so," nodded Walter. "And that's not all. We are going to get Ned Rector to join the club. He already has a pony. Wish you might come in with us, Tad."

"Wish I might," answered Tad wistfully.

"Of course, we know you can't really, but you belong to us just the same. You can be a sort of - of honorary member. We will let you ride our ponies sometimes when we are in town, though, of course, when we go out for long trips we can't take you along very well. You understand that, don't you, Tad?"

Tad inclined his head.

"And now about the name. Got anything to suggest?"

The freckle-faced boy walked over to the pony and laid his cheek against its nose, which he patted softly, his head averted so that the others might not see the pain in his eyes.

"You - you might call yourselves 'The Pony Rider Boys,'" suggested Tad, controlling his voice with an effort.

# CHAPTER II

## THE PONY RIDER BOYS' CLUB ORGANIZBD

The Pony Rider Boys, as a club, met for the purpose of organization, with headquarters under a tent in Banker Perkins's orchard. It was the tent in which Walter, under orders from the family physician, had been sleeping during the spring. Over the entrance the boys pinned a strip of canvas on which they had printed in red letters, "Headquarters Pony Rider Boys' Club."

"Now they will know who we are," explained Walter, standing off to view their handiwork. "You see, people can read that from the street. Everybody who passes will see it."

"Yes," replied Ned Rector, who already had been enrolled as a charter member. "But I hope they won't think it's a blacksmith shop over here, and drive in to get their horses shod."

The boys laughed heartily.

"The next question is, whom shall we have for president of the club?" asked Walter. "I suppose we ought to elect one to-day so we can be regularly organized."

"Yes, that's so," agreed Chunky. "What's the matter with having TadButler for president? He knows all about horses, even if he has none himself."

"But he's not a member of the club," objected Ned.

"No," agreed Walter, "but I had thought we might make him an honorary member. We ought to take him in, someway, for I know he's anxious to join us."

"Then, I would suggest that we organize first," advised Ned, who possessed some slight knowledge of parliamentary law. "You can choose one of us for temporary chairman, and then we will go ahead and form our organization just like a regular club."

"That's a good plan. Will you be the chairman, Ned?"

"No, Walt. I think I should prefer to be on the floor, where I can talk. Neither the chairman nor president has the right to argue, you know. I'm afraid I shouldn't be of much use to the club if I couldn't talk," laughed Ned. "I propose Mr. Stacy Brown, otherwise known as 'Chunky, ' for temporary chairman. Chunky is fat, and can appear very dignified when he wants to, even if he doesn't feel that way."

"That's the idea," agreed Walter.

"Now, all in favor of Mr. Chunky Brown for presiding officer of the first meeting of the Pony Rider Boys manifest it by saying 'Aye.'"

Ned and Walter voted in the affirmative.

"All opposed, say 'Nay.'"

"Nay!" voted Chunky in a loud voice.

"The Ayes have it. Mr. Stacy Chunky Brown has been duly chosen temporary chairman of the Pony Rider Boys. Mr. Chairman, will you please take the chair and call this meeting to order?" invited Ned Rector, escorting Stacy to a chair which had been placed at one end of the tent for the purpose of receiving him.

Chunky sank into the seat, gazing helplessly about him.

"Well?" urged Ned.

"Do something," laughed Walter.

"Yes, but what shall I do?"

"Call the meeting to order, of course. What do you think we elected you for? Not to sit up there and look pretty. Call it to order."

"I do."

"Help!" pleaded Ned Rector, weakly. "See here, that's not the way to do it. Is this the first time you have presided at a meeting?"

Chunky, by a nod, informed them that it was.

"Humph!" grunted Ned witheringly. "Then say after me, 'I now call the meeting of the Pony Rider Boys to order. What is your pleasure, gentlemen?'"

The chairman haltingly repeated the words.

"Now, that's the way to do it," approved Ned. "I shouldn't be surprised to see you President of the United States some day. I now move, Mr. Chairman, that Tad Butler be made an honorary member of the club, as well as riding master and manager of the live stock."

"Second the motion," added Walter quickly.

The motion was carried with much enthusiasm. Then the club voted to make Chunky Brown its permanent presiding officer, and this in spite of the winner's vigorous objections. Walter was made treasurer because, as Ned expressed it, Walter's father was a bank president. Ned Rector was chosen secretary.

"I now move," proposed Ned Rector, "that this club direct its secretary to write to the uncle of its president, pointing out to him the advisability of providing a pony for said president to ride; said president being so heavy as to make walking to the meetings of this club a burden to himself and to the club members who have to wait for him."

This motion was adopted with a shout of laughter.

After having directed the secretary, at his own suggestion, to notify Tad Butler of his election, the club adjourned to meet on the following morning for field practice. In other words, the club's two ponies, with Walter Perkins and Ned Rector upon them, were to be taken out for exercise about the village and in nearby roads.

The next day being Saturday, Tad Butler found himself too busy to devote much time to brooding over his troubles. As a matter of fact, the boy was little given to this sort of thing; he was too much a man. His was a wholesome, confident nature, and the same indomitable courage and determination that had enabled him to stand next to the head of his class in the high school filled him with a resolution to possess a pony of his own. Nor did he permit the receipt of a letter that morning, informing him of his honorary election to the Pony Riders Club, to cast him down, even though, for want of a pony, he could not enter into full membership.

Instead, with flashing eyes, his clean-cut jaw set more firmly than usual, Tad went about his duties of the day cheerfully, his active mind running over this and that plan through which he might possibly gratify his longings.

Late that same afternoon, on his way driving out to deliver a package of goods to a summer residence just outside the town, he came upon Walter and Ned, returning on their ponies from a short jaunt into the country.

The two boys hailed him joyously.

Tad grinned and waved his hand.

"Hello! Aren't you going to stop to tali with a fellow?" called Ned, as the riders came abreast of the grocery horse and pulled up.

Tad shook his head.

"Oh, come on; hold up a minute."

"Can't. I'm on business, you know," answered the boy, smiling pleasantly. "I am working all day to-day for Mr. Langdon, and I mustn't stop. I have a lot of goods to deliver before night."

"Then what do you say to our riding out and back with him, Walt?" suggested Ned.

"All right. I guess we shall have plenty of time to do that and get back for supper. Tad won't stay long. He's in too big a hurry," answered the banker's son, bringing his pony about, and galloping up beside the wagon, which had continued on its way during the conversation.

This gave Tad an opportunity to gaze admiringly at the sleek ponies on which the boys were mounted, as well as at the nickel trimmings of bridles and saddles, which glistened brightly in the sunlight.

"Wish you had him, don't you?" laughed Ned, noting Tad's gaze fixed on his own well-groomed mount.

To Ned's surprise, Tad shook his head negatively.

"Mean to tell me you don't want a pony like this?"

"I didn't say so, Ned. No, I wouldn't say that, because it isn't true. You asked me if I didn't wish I had him. Of course, I want a pony more than anything else in the world. But I want my own, not yours. That is different, you see. Much as I want one, I don't covet either yours or Walt's."

"Well, you are a funny fellow. I never did understand you," marveled Ned. "But, I guess he's about right, eh,

Walter? Don't you think so!"

"Yes. And I have been thinking, since our meeting yesterday, that perhaps it might be fixed. I wasn't going to say anything about it," answered Walter, meditatively.

"Thinking about what?" demanded Ned.

"About Tad's not having a horse, and no way to get one. I tell you, it's mighty tough -- "

"Yes?"

"Well, he is a member of the club, and as fellow members of the Pony Riders, we are bound to stand by one another."

"That's right," agreed Ned. "That's what we're going to do, too. But what are you getting at, Walt?"

Tad's blue eyes were fixed inquiringly on Walter's face. He, too, was at a loss to understand what it was that his delicate young friend was planning. Still, he would not ask, knowing full well that it was of him they were thinking.

"Simply this. Tad has got to have a pony."

Ned uttered a long-drawn whistle, while the boy on the grocery wagon suddenly straightened up.

"I agree with you there, Walt," Ned remarked. "Yet, how is he going to get one? That's what I should like to know - and it's a question that the Pony Riders will have a hard time in answering. Now, it is different with

Chunky. Chunky's uncle has money. He can well afford to buy his nephew a pony. When I went to ask him to-day he said he would see about it. That means Chunky will have one."

"Why do you think that?"

"Because my father is a lawyer, and he says when a fellow doesn't know his own mind, you can make him agree to 'most any old thing," answered Ned with a laugh.

By this time they had reached their destination. Though keenly interested in the conversation of his companions Tad leaped to the ground, tying his horse without an instant's delay, and proceeded to the house to deliver his merchandise.

The boys watched him disappear around the corner of the house before resuming their conversation.

"I'll tell you, now," began Walter. "I didn't want to explain before him. Tad is the best rider in town, you know, Ned -- "

"Next to me," added Ned humorously.

"Yes, next ahead. And he is the second best scholar in the high school. Nothing could stop him from heading the class if he had the time to devote to his studies, so Professor Zepplin tells me. I like him, Ned -- "

"Since he fished you out of the mill pond, when you fell through the ice there last winter, eh!"

"Yes, partly. But, I liked him just as well before that.

Do you know," continued Walter after a moment of silence, "I never told my father that Tad did that for me?"

"You didn't? Why not?" asked Ned, his face reflecting his surprise.

"Because Tad made me promise I wouldn't. He's such a modest chap that he didn't want father to thank him, even. So I never did -- "

"He is a queer lad -- "

"That is, I did not until last night," corrected Walter thoughtfully.

"Oh! Then you told him? What did he say?" questioned Ned, now keenly interested in the narration.

"He said Tad was a brave boy, and that he wanted to do something for him. I told him there was one thing he could do that would please me, at the same time making Tad the happiest boy in Chillicothe - yes, happier than any other boy in the state of Missouri."

"Yes?"

"Father laughed and asked me what it was that Tad desired so much." Walter glanced up at his companion, a queer smile playing about his lips.

"Well, what did you tell him!"

"That Tad wanted a pony."

The boys gazed into each other's eyes.

"Good for you," breathed Ned. "You are the right sort, even if you are weak. I always said you were. But did your father say he would get Tad a pony?"

"Well, not exactly. He wanted to know how I thought Tad could take care of a pony when he got it - said the boy would have no place to keep it, nothing to feed it on -- "

"Yes, that's so."

"But, I told him Tad might stable his pony with Jo-Jo in our barn."

"Sure thing. That's fine. Did he agree?"

"He said for me to bring Tad in to see him."

"But you did not?"

"No; I haven't had a chance. I'm going to try to get him to stop on the way back, if he will. All three of us will stop off at the bank Father usually stays late on Saturdays to go over the books all by himself -- "

Further conversation was interrupted by the return of Tad. Acting upon a knowing look from Walter, Ned maintained a discreet silence on the subject. And, if Tad's keen glance, which searched their faces, as he clambered aboard the grocery wagon, gave him the slightest inkling as to what they had been discussing, he made no effort further to gratify his curiosity.

"What are you going to do when you get back, Tad?" asked Walter by way of directing the conversation to the subject of which he was at that moment so full.

"Going back to the store. Why?"

"Oh, nothing much. Father wanted you to step in some time this afternoon," answered Walter as carelessly as he could.

"What for?"

"He wishes to talk with you about something. You can stop off as we go by. It will take only a few minutes of your time."

Tad shook his head emphatically. Nothing could deter him from doing what he considered was his full duty to his employer.

"Then I shall go over to the store with you myself and see Mr. Langdon," announced Walter firmly. After that, the conversation drifted into a discussion of the respective merits of the two ponies that Ned and Walter were riding.

Arriving at the store, Walter dismounted, and, tossing the reins to Ned, ran up the steps into the store, while Tad began methodically to haul the market baskets from the wagon, piling them together on the sidewalk.

In a moment Walter came hurrying out.

"It's all right," he called from the top step. "Mr. Langdon says hitch your horse here, while you go over with me to see father."

"Very well," replied Tad, as, with evident reluctance, he followed his friend to the bank, half a block up the street.

Mr. Perkins greeted his young guest with marked courtesy.

"Walter delayed telling me of your heroic conduct in saving his life until last night, Thaddeus. I am sorry. But, according to the old saying, 'it is never too late to mend.' Therefore, I want to thank you now."

Mr. Perkins grasped the lad's hands in a firm grip, while Tad, hiding his embarrassment as best he could, gazed with steady eyes into the face of the banker.

"I'm sorry he told you, sir. I just pulled him out - that was all."

The banker laughed.

"Yes, fortunately that was all. But there surely would have been more if you had not, Walter would have drowned. How you managed to get him out, without both of you going down, is more than I can understand."

"He dived in and swam out with me," Walter informed him.

"Quite so. And you wished my son to say nothing about it?" added the banker with a twinkle in his eyes, not wholly lost on the boy who was standing so rigidly before him, steeling himself to the most trying ordeal he ever had experienced.

"I did, sir."

"Walter respected your wishes in the matter. But something came up last evening that induced him to make a clean breast of the whole affair. And I am very glad he did so."

"Yes, sir."

"Walter tells me you are a great lover of animals, especially horses."

"I am more fond of them, sir, than of anything else in the world, save my mother," answered the boy, his eyes growing bright.

"And he also has told me about this new club of which I most heartily approve. It will be an excellent thing for Walter. But of course you will not he able to go out with the boys, not having a pony of your own."

"No, sir," answered Tad in a firm voice.

"I take it you would be very happy to be able to join them on their outings?"

"Indeed I should, Mr. Perkins."

"Well," glowed the banker, "at Walter's suggestion I have arranged it so that in the future you shall not be denied this pleasure. Do you happen to know where there are any ponies for sale at this moment?"

"Yes, sir. They have several at the McCormick farm about three miles from town. They are very fine ponies, too, sir. One of them, I think, would make an excellent mate for Jo-Jo, if you are considering getting another one for Walter to drive or ride."

"No, I was not thinking of doing that at present. I will

tell you what I propose to do, however."

"Yes, sir."

"I propose to send you out to the McCormicks' this afternoon, if you can spare the time. When you reach there you will pick out what you consider is the best pony in the lot, and bring him back to town. They will let you have him upon presentation of the letter I shall give you before you leave," smiled the banker.

"I - I don't quite understand, sir. I - I - what is it you wish me to do with the pony?" stammered Tad.

Banker Perkins rose, laying a hand on the boy's shoulder.

"Take him home with you - he is yours, Tad."

"My - my - mine?"

"Yes."

A sudden rush of color flashed into the face of Tad Butler and crept up to the roots of his hair, his eyes holding those of the hanker in an unflinching gaze.

"I - am sorry, sir; but I cannot accept it."

"What?" exclaimed Mr. Perkins.

"I thank you very much. Believe me, I do. But I could not accept a gift like that from you. You will understand me, won't you? I couldn't - I couldn't do it; that's all."

"I do, my lad. I understand you perfectly," answered the hanker slowly, grasping the lad's hand and gripping it until Tad winced.

"Thank you," murmured Tad, backing from the room, with as much composure as he was able to muster.

Reaching the street, the boy clenched his fingers until the nails dug into the palms of his hands. Then, with shoulders erect, he strode rapidly off down the street to continue his duties at the grocery store.

# CHAPTER III

## TAD GOES INTO BUSINESS

After supper, that night, Banker Perkins strolled leisurely across town to the cottage occupied by Tad Butler and his mother. The house lay on the outskirts of the village, surrounded by half an acre of ground, part of which the boy tilled, keeping the little family in vegetables a great part of the year. The rest of the plot had been seeded down, and was now covered with a bright green carpet of new clover.

Tad, being busy at the grocery store that night, did not return home for his supper, so that the banker's visit was all unknown to the boy who was going stoically about his duties over in the village. Yet, in his clear eyes there was nothing of regret at his own refusal to permit the desire of his life to be gratified.

Mr. Perkins remained at the cottage for nearly an hour and a half, and a quiet smile might have been observed hovering about his lips as he bade good-night to Mrs. Butler, whose countenance reflected something of his own satisfaction.

"I will attend to the matter on Monday morning," were his partingwords, at which Mrs. Butler bowed and withdrew into the cottage.

All unmindful of the important conference, Tad returned home at ten o'clock. His mother was awaiting him. She greeted him with a hearty embrace and a kiss, which the boy returned with no less fervor.

"I have a nice, warm supper ready for you, Tad," she informed him. "You must have a man's appetite by this time, for you have had hardly anything to eat since your breakfast."

"It does put an appetite into a fellow, riding behind a horse, even if it is an old lame one," laughed Tad.

"I really believe you would find pleasure in driving a wooden horse, such as I have seen in harness shops," smiled Mrs. Butler. "You are so like your grandfather. He would miss a meal at any time for the sake of driving a horse or talking horse with a friend."

"Father didn't care so much about them, did he?"

"No, your father was not particularly interested in horses. He was in too poor health to be able to handle them after he reached a position where he might have afforded such a luxury."

Tad nodded reflectively.

"And you still want a pony, do you, my son?" asked Mrs. Butler, leaning forward with a twinkle in her eyes. But the boy's gaze was fixed steadily on his plate and he failed to note the expression.

"Yes, I do, mother. However, I don't allow myself to think much about it. I have got to take care of you, first. After I have made enough so that you can get along, then I shall have a horse. But not until then."

"Perhaps you may have one sooner than you know," breathed the mother, veiling her eyes with her hands, that he might not read what was plainly written there.

Tad shot a keen glance at her, then resumed his supper in silence.

The subject was not again referred to between them, and on Monday afternoon Tad Butler was again at the grocery store, prepared for work should there be any for him.

Mr. Langdon, the proprietor, was talking with one of the men from his farm just outside the village.

"You say the old mare is unfit for further service, Jim?"

"Yes."

"What do you advise doing with her?"

"Shoot her."

"Very well, take the old mare out in the swamp and put her out of her misery," directed Mr. Langdon after he had thought a moment.

"I beg pardon, Mr. Langdon," interrupted Tad Butler, who had been an interested listener to the interview.

"Yes, Tad; what is it?"

"Is it old Jinny that you are speaking of, if I may ask?"

"It is," smiled the grocer, good-naturedly.

"What's the trouble with her?"

"Trouble?" sniffed the farm-hand." Jinny's got the heaves that bad she blows like a blacksmith's bellows. Why, sometimes she even coughs the oats out of her manger before she's had the chance to eat them. And that ain't all that ails her, either. I -- "

"Why do you ask, Tad?" said Grocer Langdon.

"What will you take for Jinny?" inquired the boy, the color flaming to his face as a bold plan suddenly occurred to him.

"Why, what could you do with an old, broken-down animal like that?"

"I don't know. But I should like to make a bargain with you -- "

"Of course if you want her you may have her, provided you get her off the premises at once," answered the grocer." She'll die on our hands presently, anyhow."

"No; I don't want the mare that way. But, I'll tell you what I will do, Mr. Langdon."

"Yes?"

"I will clean out your store every morning for a month in payment for the mare. Yes, I will make it two months. If two months is not long enough, I will work for you longer."

"Oh, very well. The mare's not worth it. However, if you wish to have it that way I am sure I ought to be satisfied," laughed the grocer.

"Then, will you write on a piece of paper that the mare is sold to me, and that I am to clean out the store every morning in payment for her?" asked Tad.

"Certainly, if you wish it. I wish you luck," smiled Mr. Langdon, handing the agreement over the counter after he had prepared it.

With the precious document in his pocket, Tad Butler sped homeward as fast as his legs could carry him. Mrs. Butler saw him coming and wondered what the boy's haste might mean.

"I've got a horse! I've got a horse!" shouted Tad, vaulting the fence lightly and bounding up the steps. "I surely have a horse at last, mother."

Grasping his mother about the waist with both arms, Tad whirled her dizzily, the full length of the porch and back, finally dropping her into a rocking chair with a merry laugh.

"Mercy!" gasped Mrs. Butler. "You have shaken all the breath out of me. What does this whirlwind arrival mean?"

"It means that I have a horse at last, mother. To be sure, it is not much of a horse; but it's a horse just the same. And it's all mine, too."

Mrs. Butler gazed up at him in perplexity. Tad sank down at her feet and explained the terms on which he had procured Jinny from Mr. Langdon.

"Well, now that you have her, what do you mean to do with her?" asked Mrs. Butler, a quizzical smile on her face.

"With your leave, I shall bring her home. Will you let me turn Jinny in the clover patch there, mother? There'll be enough grass there to keep her all summer, and as soon as she is able to work I can get odd jobs enough with her to pay for the oats that I shall need to keep her up on," went on the boy speaking rapidly.

"Very well, Tad; the place is as much yours as it is mine," agreed Mrs. Butler, indulgently.

"And I have been thinking of something else, too - something for you. But I shall not tell you about that now. I am going to keep it as a surprise for you when I get it ready," announced the boy mysteriously. "If you have nothing for me to do just now, I think I'll go out to Mr. Langdon's farm and bring the mare in. I shall want to spend the evening making her comfortable."

Mrs. Butler gave a ready permission, and Tad hounded away, running every foot of the mile and a half to the Langdon farm, where old Jinny was turned over to him, together with a brand new halter and an old harness which the grocer had directed his man to furnish with the mare.

Tad petted and fondled the wheezy old creature, who nosed him appreciatively.

"How old is Jinny?" he asked.

"Going on twelve," answered the farm-hand laconically.

Tad opened the mare's mouth, which he studied critically.

"Humph!" he grunted, flashing a glance of disapproval at the farm-hand.

"What's that, younker? I said as she was going on twelve."

"I guess you have dropped five years out of your reckoning somewhere," answered the boy. "Jinny is past seventeen. But it's all right. It is all the same to me. I don't care if she's a hundred," decided Tad, picking up the halter and leading the mare from the yard.

"Hope she don't run away with ye," jeered the farm-hand, as boy and horse passed out into the highway. But to this Tad made no reply. He was too fully occupied with his new happiness to allow so little a thing as the farm-hand's opinion to disturb him.

Once out of sight of the farm buildings, the lad pulled the mare to one side of the road, where he examined her carefully.

"Huh!" he exclaimed. "Heaves, ringbone and spavin. I don't know how much more is the matter with her, but that's enough. Still, I think she will wiggle along for some time and be of real service if I can fix up the heaves a little. They must have filled her up on dusty hay," he decided, examining the mare's throat and nostrils. "I'll get her home and look her over more carefully."

Tad's course led him through the principal residential street of the town. But he thought nothing of this, even though his new purchase was a mere bundle of bones and scarcely able to drag its weary body along.

"She's mine," he whispered, as the sense of possession took full hold of him. "Mine, all mine!"

Just ahead of him stood the home of Stacy Brown's uncle.

Chunky was standing in front of the gate, both hands thrust into his trousers pockets. He had observed the strange outfit coming down the street, but at first the full meaning of it did not impress him. Now he discovered that the procession consisted of Tad Butler and an emaciated, hesitating old horse.

Stacy's eyes gradually closed until they were mere slits, through which he peered inquiringly.

"Hullo, Tad," he greeted.

"Hello, Chunky," returned the freckle-faced boy with a grin.

"What you got there, a skeleton?"

"No; this is a mare. Her name is Jinny and she's mine."

"Huh! Skate, I call her. Where did you get her?"

"Bought her," answered Tad proudly.

Chunky emitted a long-drawn whistle.

"What are you going to do with her?" he demanded, a sudden suspicion entering his mind.

"First, I am going to doctor her up and make a real live horse of her. Then, perhaps, she will join the Pony Riders' Club."

"What?"

"I said she might join the club," reiterated Tad.

"Then I resign," declared Chunky.

"All right," retorted Tad. "Jinny's better than no horse at all. And you haven't any."

"Yes, but my uncle is going to get me one next week. He's going to buy the handsomest one he can find out at the McCormick ranch," chortled the fat boy.

"Gid-ap!" commanded Tad, his face sobering. "I don't care. I'll show them yet," he gritted, urging old Jinny along with sundry coaxes and promises of a real meal upon their arrival home.

Though the boy tried to keep his purchase a secret until he should have conditioned the mare a little, Stacy Brown lost no time in informing the other members of the club, and through them the news soon became the property of the village. As a result, Tad was the butt of many jokes and jibes, to all of which he returned a quiet smile, registering a mental promise to "show them."

In two weeks time he had worked a marvelous change in Jinny. One who had seen her on the day the boy brought her home, would scarcely have recognized in her the old, wind-broken skeleton that she had appeared two weeks previously.

By this time, Tad was beginning to use her to haul up wood which he had gathered in a patch of forest below the village. He would first gather and pile the poles; then, wrapping a rope about all he thought the mare could draw, would make her haul them home. Here he sawed the poles to stove lengths in preparation for the winter. This work Mrs. Butler had always been obliged to hire done, and the saving now was of no small moment to her.

One hot afternoon, however, Tad had left Jinny in the shade of the trees to rest, while he wandered out to the highway and sat down to think.

He had been there not more than fifteen minutes when the faint chug, chug of a motor car was borne to his ears. It was still some distance away, but from the sound he knew the car was approaching rapidly.

"If they keep on at that gait, something surely will happen," decided Tad, being fully aware of the dangers that lay in the stretch of road between himself and the oncoming car.

A few moments later he saw the car round the bend in the road just beyoud him. It came tearing along, swerved unsteadily from one side of the road to the other, then was brought to a sudden, grinding stop, narrowly missing a plunge into the roadside ditch.

"The steering gear has gone wrong. I think the ball has been wrenched from the socket," announced the driver of the car, disgustedly. "I wish I could see a horse."

Tad grinned.

"What are you grinning at, you young ape?" snapped the driver, voicing his increasing irritation. "You seem to think this is some kind of a joke."

"I am not laughing at you, sir," answered Tad respectfully.

"You'd better not," growled the driver. "How far is it to Chillicothe, kid?"

"About a mile and a half," replied the boy.

"Can I get a horse anywhere around here?"

"I reckon you can. I've got a horse."

"You? Where is it?" demanded the autoist doubtfully.

"In the bushes, back here a piece. What'll you give me to pull you in?"

"I'll give you five dollars," announced the driver eagerly. "But be quick about it."

Tad rose slowly and stretched himself.

"I'll do it for two," he announced, to the surprise and amusement of the occupants of the car.

In a few moments Jinny had been led out, Tad taking

along the rope that he used in hauling the wood. One end he fastened securely to the front axle of the car, attaching the other to the whiffletree that he had made to use in the woods.

"Now, if you will start your engine and give me just a little lift, I think I can draw you in. Can you steer the car enough to keep it in the road, do you think?"

"I will try," answered the driver. "But if I find I can't, I'll toot my horn, which will be the signal for you to stop."

It was all the old mare could do to draw the heavy car over the slight rise of ground that lay just beyond where the automobile had been stalled; yet, with the aid of the power of the car itself, they managed to make the hill all right. At last the boy pulled the car and its occupants up in front of the blacksmith shop in the village, collecting his fee with the air of one used to transacting similar business every day.

Tad, however, did not return to the woods that day. Instead, he turned old Jinny toward home, which he made all haste to reach.

Arriving there he placed the money he had earned in his mother's hands.

"Just earned it with Jinny," he explained proudly, in answer to her surprised look. "I'll get the wood to-morrow, and maybe I'll catch another automobile."

However, Tad's luck deserted him next day, though three days later he earned a dollar and a half towing in a disabled car.

This led the lad to ponder deeply, the result being a hurried trip to the store, followed by sundry mysterious preparations in the stable at the rear of the house.

Tad's early mornings were devoted to cleaning up the store, so that he had no time then to give to his own affairs. Late one afternoon in the middle of the following week, Tad Butler, driving Jinny and with a parcel under his arm, moved down the street toward the woods.

Arriving at the woods he tied Jinny to a tree and walked on around a bend in the highway, where he unrolled his parcel. A coil of clothes line dropped from it.

The bundle, which proved to be a long strip of canvas, Tad stretched out, tying an end of the clothes line on either side.

The boy's next move was to climb a tree at one side of the road, and make fast one of the lines. Descending, he did the same on the opposite side of the highway.

By this time, Tad's clothes were in a sad state of disorder. But to this he gave no heed. He was bent on accomplishing a certain purpose, and all else must give way before it.

Hauling down on the rope which he had made fast to the second tree, be caused a banner to flutter to the breeze directly over the highway. On it in big red letters had been painted:

AUTOS TOWED IN.
IF YOU DON'T SEE ANY ONE,

YELL FOR TAD OR CALL
AT LANGDON'S STORE.
TOW YOU IN FOR TWO DOLLARS.

"I guess that's high enough to clear a load of hay,"
decided Tad, standing off and critically, surveying his
work.

# CHAPTER IV

## A SURPRISE, INDEED

That makes fifteen dollars, mother. Tad Butler, with flashing eyes and heightened color, laid two crisp new one dollar bills in his mother's hand, and nervously brushed a shock of hair from his forehead.

"My, that car was a big one," he continued." Jinny couldn't quite pull it, so I had to get behind and push. But we made it."

Mrs. Butler patted the disorderd hair affectionately.

"Need a comb, don't I?" he grinned. "Now, I am going to tell you about the surprise I promised you, Mother. I've pieced together that old broken down buggy out in the barn, and, when I can afford to buy some paint for it, you will have a carriage to ride in. You needn't be ashamed of it, for it's a dandy. Nobody will know it from a new one. Then, when I am at school, you and Jinny can go out for a drive every day. Come out and look at it, Mother, please."

Proudly escorting his mother to the stable, Tad exhibited the vehicle that he had spent many nights putting together. It was truly a creditable piece of work, and Mrs. Butler made her son happy by telling him so.

Tad's business venture had proved more profitable than even he had dreamed, and the owners of cars breaking down on the rough road made frequent use of the invitation extended on the sign. Soon, however, there were so many calls during the day, when the young man was at school, that he was considering the advisability of taking in a partner who would attend to the towing when he was not available. The only reason Tad hesitated was because he feared his assistant would not be considerate of Jinny. Yet this, he told himself, should not deter him from making the move the moment he found the right sort of a boy to go in with him.

During the past week there had been frequent conferences between Mrs. Butler and Banker Perkins, and on several occasions Tad's mother had called at the hank in person. Of all this the young man knew nothing. But one afternoon something did occur to stir him more profoundly than he ever had been stirred before.

Ned Rector had called a meeting of the Pony Rider Boys, and the word was passed that important business was coining up for discussion.

Tad said he could not spare the time from his business down the road.

"I wish you would take the afternoon off," advised his mother. "You have been working hard of late, and I imagine the boys will have something to discuss that will be of great interest to you," added Mrs. Butler with a knowing smile.

"W-e-l-l," answered Tad. "If you think I ought to, of course I will. "What are you going to do?"

"I am going out to take tea with Mrs. Secor. I will leave your supper in the oven and you can help yourself. Besides, it will do Jinny fully as much good as it will you to have a rest. Have you seen Mr. Perkins to-day?"

"No. Why?"

"He said something about wanting you to drop in soon, when I saw him downtown this morning," answered Mrs. Butler softly. "Now, run along and attend your important meeting, my boy."

"All right," answered Tad cheerily, after a second's hesitation. He ran lightly from the house, whistling a merry tune as he went.

Arriving at the headquarters of the club, he found all the members there awaiting him.

"Hello! How's the skate!" they cried in chorus.

"Howdy, fellows," greeted the freckle-faced lad with a pleased smile. "Jinny goes when the automobile doesn't. Give me a horse every time. How's the new pony, Chunky? Been too busy to drop in to look him over."

"I fell off yesterday," replied Stacy Brown with a sheepish grin.

"That's no news," jeered Ned Rector. "I guess we'll have to get a net for Chunky to perform over.

However, fellows, as the notice stated, we have some very, very important matters to talk over to-day. President Brown will please take his chair and call the meeting to order. That is, if he is able to sit down. If not, I think there will be no objection to his standing up," announced Ned, amid a general laugh.

The president rapped sharply on the floor with his foot, and the members of the club settled down to the keenest attention. Anticipation was reflected on each smiling face. Tad instinctively felt that there was something behind all of this that he knew nothing about. But he bided his time.

"What is the pleasure of the meeting?" asked the president.

"I move," said Ned Rector, "that our friend and fellow member, Walter Perkins, now take the floor and outline the plans which I understand he has in mind. I think none of us know what they are, beyoud the fact that some sort of a trip has been planned for us. We are all ears, Mr. Perkins."

Walter rose with great deliberation, a smile playing over his thin, pale features, as he looked quietly from one to the other of his young friends.

"Fellow members," he began.

"Hear, hear!" muttered Ned.

Stacy Brown dug his heel into the floor for order.

"As brother Rector already has said, we are soon to take a trip. The matter has all been arranged. In the first place, our doctor says that I must spend the summer in the open air - that I must rough it, you understand. The rougher the life, the better it will be for me. He didn't say so to me, but I overheard him telling father that I was liable to have consumption, if I did not -- "

"You don't mean it?" interrupted Ned with serious face.

"Yes. That's what he said. So they have planned a trip for me and all of you boys are to go along."

"Hooray!" shouted Chunky.

Ned fixed him with a stern eye.

"A president never should forget his dignity," he warned. "Mr. Perkins will now proceed."

"We all now have our ponies, except Tad Butler, and when we get ready to start we shall have nothing to do but go. Professor Zepplin is to accompany us. Father has bought him a big new cob horse. The professor was once an officer in the German army, and he knows how to ride - that is, the way they ride over there. He reminds me of a statue on horseback, when he's up. Anyhow, he will go along to see that we are taken care of."

"When do we go?" asked the president.

"As soon after your school closes as is possible."

"I am afraid our fathers and uncles will have something to say about that," said Chunky with a wry face. "Uncle never would let me go off like that. It's all very well for you, but with the rest of us it's different."

Walter smiled knowingly.

"That has all been taken care of, fellows. Tour fathers, as well as mine, know all about it."

"You don't mean it?" marveled Ned.

"Yes."

"Is Tad Butler going on that old skate of his?" bristled Chunky.

"I can't say as to that," answered Walter.

"Well, if he does, it's me for home. Why, we never would get beyoud the water works station, he would he so slow. Does my uncle know about Tad's old mare?"

"Never mind about the mare," growled Ned Rector. "We have other and more important matters to attend to just now."

"Yes, and we shall have to settle among ourselves what we are to take along, though father said he had a man who would look out for all that. We are going to rough it, you understand, so we shall have to leave behind all our fine clothes. And sometimes we may go without meals, even. But we all will sleep out-of-doors, most likely, every night after we get started. In the meantime, I would suggest that we practice riding - that is, form ourselves into a sort of company with a regular captain. I move that Tad Butler be made captain, and he can drill us."

"You don't need to make that motion," announced Ned, springing to his feet, full of excitement. "He will be our captain without being elected. He already is master of horse. It's now up to Tad to get busy and drill us. We will begin to-morrow afternoon."

Tad, who had taken no part in the conversation, now shook his head slowly, which caused the others to shout in chorus:

"You won't!"

"Of course I will drill you, if you boys wish it. But, you know I can't go with you. Therefore, you had tetter make some one of you three fellows the captain."

"Why can't you go?" demanded Ned Rector. "Of course you are going."

"In the first place, I am too busy," answered Tad with a wan smile. "Then there are other reasons. I can't afford it. I must stay at home and earn money this summer. Then, again, I have no pony."

"Oh pshaw!" growled Ned. "That's too bad. I would rather stay at home myself."

Tad flashed an appreciative glance at him.

"Thank you. But I would rather you went, Ned. I'll drill you willingly if you boys want me to."

"That's right," approved Walter. "Perhaps something may turn up in the meantime, so you can go with us. It really will spoil our trip if you don't go along."

"Nothing will turn up. Nothing can turn up. I tell you, I must stay at home with my mother. But I don't even know where you are going. I can drill you to better purpose if I know what sort of riding you expect to do."

"Yes! Where are we going?" demanded Chunky, with quickened interest.

"That's so. I hadn't thought of that. Where did your father say we were to ride to? We must be going quite a distance away, judging by all the preparations," besought Ned Rector. "And, by the way, are you sure you are right about this business, Walt?"

"There is no doubt," smiled Walter Perkins good-naturedly. "That is what this meeting was called for - to tell you about it. It was left to me to announce it to you boys, because it is my party, if you want to call it that. And you want to know where you are going?"

"Yes, of course we do," they shouted.

"Boys, we are going to the Rocky Mountains! We are going over the roughest and wildest part of them. Perhaps we shall go where no white man's foot ever has trod. We shall be explorers. What do you think of it?"

For a full moment no one spoke.

Each was too full of the wonderful news to do more than gape at the speaker. Only the sound of their labored breathings broke the stillness.

"Will - will there be bears and things there?" asked

Stacy, hesitatingly.

"I presume so," smiled Walter.

"Ugh! And snakes?"

"Maybe."

"Rattlers. I've read about them out there," added Ned.

"I - I guess I'll stay home," stammered the president.

"Don't be a baby," jeered Ned. "I rather think you'll be able to stand it if the rest of us can. And, besides, Walt's professor will be along. He'll fix the animals and reptiles with, his cold, scientific eye till they'll be glad to run away and leave us to ourselves."

"You boys are to come over to my house tomorrow night, when father is going to tell you more about it. He has not told me everything yet. But he directed me to give you the main points of the plan, which I have done."

"I propose three cheers for Walter Perkins and his father," cried Ned, springing to his feet. The boys joined in the cheers with a will, Tad no less loudly than the rest, though there was no joy in his face now. The boy's disappointment was keen, yet he determined that his friends should not see it. And, as quickly as he could do so, Tad slipped away and went home to fight out his boyish sorrow all alone.

Tad's mother found him out in the barn half an hour later, vigorously grooming the old mare. Mrs. Butler smiled to herself as she observed that he studiously managed to keep the mare between himself and her as he worked.

"Do you want to sell Jinny?" she asked after a little.

"What?"

Tad was all attention now.

"I said, do you want to sell your horse?"

"No. That is, I might if I got enough for her. But I can't say that I am anxious to. Why, I am making plenty of money with her," answered Tad coining out from behind the mare. "What made you ask that question, Mother?"

"I didn't know but you might be willing to part with her. And then, with the money you might be able to purchase a better one - a horse that you would be able to earn more money with."

Tad studied his mother's face a moment inquiringly.

"Not with any money that I could get for Jinny."

"How much do you think you could get for her?"

"Not more than ten dollars. I doubt if any one would be willing to pay that, even. Who wants to buy her?"

"Yes; Mr. Secor, the butcher, spoke to me about it while I was at his house this afternoon. His delivery horse broke a leg yesterday and they had to shoot the animal to-day."

"Too bad," muttered Tad.

"He thought Jinny was just the horse he wanted, because she is so gentle and will stand without hitching. It takes too much time to hitch a delivery horse at every stop, you know!"

Tad nodded his understanding.

"Did you tell him what ailed Jinny?" asked Tad.

"Yes, as well as I could. But he said he knew all about her, and was willing to take all chances. Mr. Secor said he believed Jinny was good for ten years yet, with the kind of work he would require of her."

"Make an offer?" asked Tad, with an eye to business.

"Yes."

"How much?"

"Twenty-five dollars."

"W-h-e-w! He must be crazy. All right, he can have her so far as I am concerned. I'll go over to see him this evening."

That night Tad Butler came home with twenty-five dollars in his pocket, which, added to what he already had earned, made the tidy sum of forty dollars - a little fortune for him.

He dropped the handful of bills into his mother's lap, and, going out to the porch, sat down with his head in his hands, to think. Mrs. Butler followed him after a few moments.

"Do you think you would like to go with the boys on their jaunt this summer?" she asked, innocently enough, it seemed.

"Yes, but I can't."

"Why not, my boy?"

"First place, I've got no pony."

"Don't be too sure about that"

"What do you mean, Mother!"

"Run out to the stable and see," smiled Mrs. Butler.

Wonderingly, Tad did as she had directed. And there in a stall stood a sleek Indian Texas pony, quite the finest little animal he had ever seen.

"Wh - whe - where did he come from!" gasped the astonished boy.

"You earned him, Tad, and the money you brought home this evening will complete the purchase price. You shall accompany the Pony Riders on their trip to the Rockies -- "

"But -- "

"Mr. Perkins has arranged to have you go with Walter to look after him. You will be his companion, and for this service Mr. Perkins agrees to pay you the sum of five dollars a week and all expenses. Understand, you are not going as a servant - he wished that made very clear - but as the young man's companion. You can easily get someone to do your work at the store for another month, when your agreement will be worked out."

"Yes - but - but you, Mother?"

"I am invited to spend the summer with Aunt Jane, so you need have no concern whatever about me."

Tad's eyes grew large as the full significance of it all was home in upon him.

"Mother, you're a brick," he cried, impulsively throwing his arms about Mrs. Butler.

But Tad had no thought of the thrilling experiences through which he was destined to pass during the coming eventful journey.

# CHAPTER V

## IN A DESPERATE CONFLICT

A sudden bright flash lighted up the camp, throwing the little white tents into hold relief against the sombre background of the mountains. It was followed after an interval by a low rumble of distant thunder that buffeted itself from peak to peak of the Rockies.

The Pony Riders stirred restlessly on their cots and tucked the blankets up under their chins.

Close upon the first report followed another and louder one, that sent a distinct tremor through the mountain.

"What's that?" whispered Stacy Brown, reaching from his cot and grasping Tad Butler by the shoulder.

"A mountain storm coming up," answered the boy, who for some time had lain wide awake listening to the ever increasing roar. "Go to sleep."

Yet, instead of following his own advice, Tad lay with wide-open eyes awaiting the moment when the storm should descend upon their camp in full force.

He had not long to wait.

With a crash and a roar, as if the batteries of an army had been suddenly let loose upon them, the elements opened their bombardment directly over the camp.

"Ugh!" exclaimed Chunky in a muffled voice, as he crawled further down under the blanket to shut out the glare of the lightning.

For a few moments the boys lay thus. Then Tad, rising, slipped to the opening of the tent and looked out wonderingly upon the impressive scene. Each flash appeared to light up the mountains for miles around, their crests lying dark and forbidding, piled tier upon tier, the blue, menacing flashes hovering about them momentarily, then fading away in the impenetrable darkness.

The camp appeared to be wrapped in sleep, and, by the bright flashes, Tad observed that the burros of the pack train were stretched out sound asleep, while, off in the bushes, he could hear the restless moving about of the ponies, their slumbers already disturbed by the coming of the storm.

The Pony Riders had been out three days from Pueblo, to which point they had journeyed by train, the stock having been shipped there in a stable car attached to the same train. In the city of Pueblo they found that all preparations for the journey had been made by Lige Thomas, the mountain guide whom Mr. Perkins had engaged to accompany them.

Besides the four ponies of the boys there were the Professor's cob, Thomas's pony and a pack train consisting of six burros, the latter in charge of Jose, a half-breed Mexican, who was to cook for the party during their stay in the mountains.

It was a brave and joyous band that had set out from the Colorado city in khaki trousers, blue shirts and broad-brimmed sombreros for an outing over the wildest of the Rocky Mountain ranges.

By this time the boys had learned to pitch and strike camp in the briefest possible time - in short, to take very good care of themselves under most of the varying conditions which such a life as they were leading entailed.

They had made camp this night on a rooky promontory, under clear skies and with bright promise for the morrow.

Tad gave a quick start as a flash of lightning disclosed something moving on the far side of the camp.

"What's that!" he breathed.

With quick intuition, the boy stepped back behind the flap of the tent, and, peering out, waited for the next flash with eyes fixed upon the spot where he thought he had observed something that did not belong there.

"Humph! I must be imagining things tonight," he muttered, when, after three or four illuminations, he had discovered nothing further.

Tad was about to return to his cot when his attention was once more attracted to the spot. And what he saw this time thrilled him through and through.

A man was cautiously leading two of the ponies from

camp, just back of Professor Zepplin's tent.

The boy paused with one hand raised above his head, prepared to pull the tent flap quickly back in place in case the stranger chanced to glance that way, all the while gazing at the man with unbelieving eyes.

Was he dreaming? Tad wondered, pinching himself to make sure that he really was awake.

Once more, impenetrable darkness settled over the scene, and, when the next flash came the camp had resumed its former appearance.

Tad Butler hesitated only for the briefest instant.

"Ahoy, the camp!" he shouted at the top of his voice, springing out into the open. "Wake up! Wake up!"

As if to accentuate his alarm, a twisting gust of wind swooped down upon the white village. Accompanied by the sound of breaking ropes and ripping canvas, the tent that had covered Professor Zepplin was wrenched loose. It shot up into the air, disappearing over a cliff.

Now the lightning flashes were incessant, and the thunder had become one continuous, deafening roar.

Stoical as he was, the Professor, thus rudely awakened, uttered a yell and leaped from his cot, while the boys of the party came tumbling from their blankets, rubbing their eyes and demanding in confused shouts to know what the row was about.

But Lige, experienced mountaineer that he was, instinctively divined the cause of the uproar, when, emerging from his tent, he saw Tad darting at top speed across the camp ground.

"The ponies! The ponies!" shouted the boy, as he disappeared in the bushes, regardless of the fact that he was clad only in his pajamas, and that the sharp rocks were cutting into his bare feet like keen-edged blades.

"What about the ponies?" roared Ned Rector, quickly collecting his wits and following in the wake of the fleeing Tad.

"Stolen! Two of them gone!" was the startling announcement thrown back to them by the freckle-faced boy.

By this time the entire camp, with the exception of Professor Zepplin and Stacy Brown, had set out on a swift run, following on the trail of Tad.

Ahead of him, the boy could hear the ponies' hoofs on the rocks, and now and then a distant crash told him they were working up into the dense second growth that he had seen in his brief tour of inspection earlier in the evening. He realized from the sound that he was slowly gaining on the missing animals.

Tad's blood was up. His firm jaw assumed the set look that it had shown when he won the championship wrestling match at the high school.

The shouts of the others at his rear, warning him of the danger and calling upon him to return, fell upon unheeding ears. So intent was the boy upon the accomplishment of his purpose that he gave no heed to the fact that the sounds ahead had ceased, and that only the soft patter of his own feet on the rocks broke the stillness between the loud claps of thunder.

Yet, even if Tad had sensed this, its meaning doubtless would have been lost upon him, unused as he was to the methods of mountaineers. So the boy ran blindly on in brave pursuit of the man who had stolen their mounts while the Pony Riders slept.

Suddenly, without the slightest warning, Tad felt himself encircled by a pair of powerful arms, and, at the same time, he was lifted clear of the ground.

But even then the lad's presence of mind did not desert him, though the vise-like pressure about his body made him gasp.

All his faculties were instantly on the alert. But he realized now that his only hope lay in attracting the attention of the others of his party, who could be only a short distance away, for he could still hear their shouts.

"Help!"

Tad's shrill voice punctuated a momentary lull in the storm.

"Coming!" answered the voice of the guide, its strident tones carrying clearly to Tad, filling him with a feeling as near akin to joy as was possible under the circumstances.

With a snarl of rage the boy's captor suddenly released his hold around the waist and grasped Tad quickly by the knees. So skilfully had the move been executed that Tad Butler found himself dangling, head down, before he really understood what had occurred. His head was whirling dizzily. He felt his body swaying from side to side, his head describing an arc of a circle, as he was rapidly being swung to and fro.

"Where are you, Tad?"

"Here!" came the muffled voice of the boy, too low for the others to catch.

Tad knew that they would have to hurry if they were to save him, for as soon as the dizzy swinging of his body began he had understood the purpose of his captor. At any second the boy might find himself flying through space - perhaps over a precipice. It plainly was the intent of the man to hurl the boy far from him, as soon as Tad's body should have attained sufficient momentum to carry it.

However, before the fellow was able to put his desperate plan fully into execution, Tad, with the resourcefulness of a born wrestler, suddenly formed a plan of his own.

As his body swung by that of his captor, the boy threw out his hands, clasping them about the left leg of the other and instantly locking his fingers.

It seemed as if the jolt would wrench his arms from their sockets. Yet Tad held on desperately. And the result, though wholly unexpected by the mountaineer, was not entirely so to Tad. He had figured - had hoped - that a certain thing might occur. And it did.

The man's left leg was jerked free of the ground, and before he was able to catch his balance the fellow fell heavily on his side. Tad, with keen satisfaction, heard him utter a grunt as he struck. But before the boy could release himself he was grabbed and pulled up over his adversary by the latter's left hand, his right still being pinioned under his own body. Yet the mountaineer's move had not been entirely without results favorable to his captive.

"I'll kill you for this!" snarled the man, fuming with rage.

Tad, groping for a wrestler's hold, felt his hand close over the hilt of a knife in the man's belt. And, as the boy was hauled upward, the blade came away from its sheath, clasped in Tad's firm grip.

But not even with this deadly weapon in hand did Tad Butler for a second forget himself. He flung the knife as far from him as his partly pinioned arms would permit, and, with keen satisfaction, heard it clatter on the rocks several feet away.

"You'll do it without that cowardly weapon, then!" gasped the boy.

Though thoroughly at home in a wrestling game, Tad knew that he would he no match for the superior strength of his antagonist. So, resorting to every wrestling trick that he knew, he sought to prevent the fellow from getting the right arm free. However, the most the lad could hope to accomplish would be to delay the dreaded climax for a minute or more.

With an angry, menacing growl, the mountaineer threw himself on his hack, hoping thereby to free the pinioned arm.

"Now, I've got you, you young cub!"

Instantly, both of Tad's knees were drawn up and forced down with all his strength on his adversary's stomach. From the growl of rage that followed, Tad had the satisfaction of knowing that his tactics had not been without effect.

"You - you only think you have," retorted the boy, breathing heavily under the terrible strain.

The mountaineer might now have hurled the boy from him. To do this, however, would have been giving Tad an opportunity to escape, of which he would have been quick to take advantage; and so, gulping quick, short breaths, and struggling with his slightly built adversary, Tad's captor finally managed to throw the lad over on his back.

So heavily did Tad strike that, for the moment, the breath was fairly knocked from his body.

Recovering himself with an effort, he raised a piercing call for help.

All grew black about him. He no longer saw the brilliant flashes of lightning that at intervals lighted up the scene, nor heard the voices of his companions frantically calling upon him to come back. The mountaineer's sinewy fingers had closed in an iron-grip over Tad Butler's throat.

# CHAPTER VI

## THE CAPTURE OP THE HORSE THIEF

"There they are!" cried Ned Rector, a flash of lightning having disclosed the man kneeling over Tad Butler. "He's got Tad down!"

But Lige Thomas did not even hear the warning words. He, too, during the momentary illumination, had caught the significance of the scene.

With a mighty leap he hurled himself upon the body of the crouching mountaineer, both going down in a confused heap, with the unfortunate Tad underneath.

Ned Rector was only a few seconds behind the guide. While the two men were straggling in fierce embrace, he sprang to them, and, grabbing Tad by the heels, drew him from beneath the bodies of the desperate combatants. But Ned's heart sank when he saw Lige drop over backward, with the mountaineer on top.

With a courage born of the excitement of the moment, Ned clasped both hands under the fellow's chin, jerking his head violently backwards. So sudden was the jolt that the lad distinctly heard the man's neck snap, and, for the moment, believed he had broken it entirely.

However, the mountaineer's tough coating of muscle made such a result impossible. Yet he had sustained a jolt so severe that, for the time being, he found himself absolutely helpless, and wholly at the mercy of his antagonists.

Lige leaped upon the thief with the lightness of a cat, quickly completing the job which Ned Rector had begun. In a moment more the guide had thrown several strands of tough rawhide lariat about the body of the dazed mountaineer, binding the fellow's arms tightly to his side.

"I guess that will hold him for a while," laughed Ned. Then, bethinking himself of Tad, whom in the excitement of conflict he had entirely forgotten, Rector dropped down beside his comrade.

"Tad! Tad! Are you all right?"

Tad made no response. He told Ned afterwards that he had heard him distinctly, though to save his life he could not have answered.

Ned pulled him up into a sitting posture, and shook the boy until his teeth chattered. Tad gulped and began to choke, his breath beginning to come irregularly.

"How's the boy?" demanded the guide, rising after having completed his task of binding the captive.

"He'll he all right in a minute. Is there any water about here!"

"No; not nearer than the camp. Wait a minute; I'll bring him around without it," announced Lige.

In this case, however, Tad felt that the remedy was considerably worse than the disease itself. Lige brought his brawny hand down with a resounding whack, squarely between Tad's shoulders, which operation he repeated several times with increasing force.

"On - ouch!" yelled Tad, suddenly finding his voice under the guide's heroic treatment. "Wh - where am I?"

"You're in the woods. That's about all I know about it," laughed Ned, assisting his companion to his feet, and supporting him, for Tad was still a bit unsteady from his late desperate encounter. "You're lucky to be alive."

"What - what has happened!"

"That," answered Ned, pointing to Lige as the latter roughly jerked the captive mountaineer to an upright position.

"Find the ponies!" commanded the guide sharply. "I hear them in the bushes there. Will they come if you whistle!"

"Depends upon which ones they are. Mine will."

But, though Ned whistled vigorously, neither of the animals appeared to heed the signal.

"Jimmie isn't there. I'll go get them." And Ned ran off into the bushes, where they could hear him coaxing the little animals to him. In a few moments he returned leading them by their bridle reins.

"Whose ponies are they?" asked Tad, leaning against a tree for support.

"Texas and Jo-Jo. The fellow picked a couple of good ones. But then, all the ponies are worth having," added Ned, realizing that he was placing the others ahead of his own little animal. "What do you propose to do with that fellow over there, guide?"

"Depends upon you young gentlemen. Just now I am going to tie him on one of the ponies and take him back to camp. I suppose you know what they do with hoss thieves in this country, don't you?" asked Thomas.

"Never having been a horse thief, and never having caught one, I can't say that I do," confessed Master Ned. "What do they do with them?"

"Depends upon whether there are any large trees about," answered Lige significantly. "We must be getting back now. Master Tad, you get on your pony, and I will lead Jo-Jo behind with the thief."

The mountaineer had been securely tied to the back of Walter Perkins's mount, and the procession now quickly got under way, Tad riding ahead, Ned Rector bringing up the rear, that he might keep a wary eye on their prisoner on their way back to camp. Ned was armed with a club, a stout limb of oak, which he had picked up before the start, and which he covertly hoped he might have an opportunity to use before reaching camp.

However, no such chance was given him, and, after picking their way cautiously over the rocky way, for trail there was none, they at last reached their temporary home.

Ned gave a war whoop as a signal to the camp that they were coming, which was answered with a slightly lesser degree of enthusiasm by Stacy Brown.

The storm had died down to a distant roar and the camp was in darkness.

"Get a fire going as quickly as possible," directed the guide.

Ned quickly procured dry fuel, and in a few moments had a crackling fire burning.

Professor Zepplin and Stacy Brown now came forward into the circle of light. After the sudden departure of his tent the Professor had taken refuge in one of the other tents, where he had remained, not knowing exactly what had happened.

In the excitement of losing his own little home he did know that all the boys, save Stacy, had rushed out of camp, shouting about the theft of the ponies. Chunky averred that all the stock had run away. Still there seemed nothing left for the two to do except remain where they were until the return of the others of the party. They would have been sure to lose themselves had they ventured away from camp in the darkness.

Both paused suddenly when they observed the figure of a man tied to the back of Jo-Jo.

"What's this? What's this?" demanded the Professor in puzzled accents. "A man tied to a horse? What is the meaning of this, sir?"

Lige Thomas smiled grimly.

"That's our prisoner," declared Tad, who, sitting upon his horse in his bedraggled, torn pajamas, presented a most ludicrous figure.

"You certainly are a sight, sir," declared Professor Zepplin, surveying the boy with disapproving eyes. "What is the meaning of all this disturbance? First, my tent goes up into the air; then you all disappear, though where I am not advised. And now, you return with a man tied to a pony."

"The man's a thief - " began Ned.

"It was this way, Professor," Tad informed him. "I saw some one walking away with Jo-Jo and Texas. I ran after and caught up with the fellow. Then the others came and we nabbed him. That's all."

"Yes, sir; if it hadn't been for Master Tad's quickness we might have lost both the ponies," added the guide. "He caught the fellow and handled him as well as a man could have done until we got there. When you get your full strength, you'll be a whirlwind, young man," glowed Lige.

Blushing, Tad slipped from his pony.

"The man is a thief, you say, Thomas?"

"Yes, sir."

"Well, well; I am surprised. I should like to take a look

at him."

Thomas dumped the prisoner on the ground in the full glare of the torches, still leaving his arms bound, and taking the further precaution of securing the fellow's feet.

"Who are you, my man!" demanded the Professor sternly, peering down into the prisoner's dark, sullen face.

There was no response.

"Humph! Can't he talk, Thomas?"

"I reckon he can, but he won't," grinned Lige. "There ain't no use in asking him questions. He knows we've caught him in the act, and he knows, too, what the penalty is."

"The penalty - the penalty? You refer to imprisonment, of course?"

"No; that ain't what I mean."

"Then, to what penalty do you refer?" inquired the Professor.

"We usually hang a hoss thief in this country," replied the guide, grimly. "But, of course, it's for you and the boys to say what shall be done."

"Hang him? Hang him? Certainly not! How can you suggest such a thing? We will turn him over to the officers of the law, and let them dispose of him in the regular way," declared the Professor with emphasis.

"That's all right, but where are we going to find any officers?" asked Tad. "They don't seem to be numerous about here."

"The young gentleman has hit the bull's-eye, sir. It's sixty miles, and more, to a jail. You don't want to go back, do you?"

"Certainly not."

"That's how we men of the mountains come to take the law into our own hands, sometimes. We have to be officers and jails, all in one," hinted the guide significantly.

"Then, there remains only one thing for us to do, regrettable as it may seem," decided the Professor after a moment's thought.

"Yes, sir?"

"Let the fellow go, but with the admonition not to offend again."

Lige laughed.

"Heap he'll care about that," he retorted, his, face growing glum.

However, at the Professor's direction, the prisoner was liberated. No sooner was this done than the fellow leaped to his feet and started to run.

"Catch him!" roared Lige.

Tad promptly stuck out a foot. The mountaineer

tripped over it, measuring his length on the ground. Lige jerked the fellow to his feet and stood him against a tree, the thief becoming suddenly meek when he found himself looking along the barrel of a large six-shooter.

"I reckon you can run now, if you want to," grinned the guide suggestively.

"Admonish him," urged the Professor.

"Now, you see here, fellow," said Lige in a menacing tone, "you've struck a rich find tonight. Next time, I reckon you won't get off so easy. I've got you marked. I'll find out what your brand is, then I'll tell the sheriff to be on the lookout for you. Now, you hit the trail as fast as your legs'll carry you. If I catch you up to any more tricks - well, you know the answer. Now, git!"

And the late prisoner did. One bound carried him almost out of camp. The boys shouted derisively as they heard him floundering through the bushes as he hastily made his escape.

"Where is Walt? Did he go hack to bed?" asked Tad, after the excitement had subsided.

"To bed? No; he followed you," replied Stacy Brown.

"Followed us? You are mistaken. Did you see anything of Walter Perkins, Mr. Thomas?"

The guide shook his head.

"Did not go with you? I think you must be in error,"

spoke up the Professor, with quick concern.

"He certainly was not with us," insisted Ned. "I did not even see him leave his tent."

"Why, he must have gone. With my own eyes I saw him running after you," urged Professor Zepplin in a tone of great anxiety.

"Guide, get torches at once. The boy surely is lost."

Alarmed, the boys needed no further incentive to spur them to instant action. Grasping fagots from the fire, they lined up, standing with anxious faces, awaiting the direction of Lige Thomas, to whom they instinctively looked to command the searching party.

"Wait a minute," commanded Lige in a calm voice. "Which way did you see him go, Professor?"

"Let me reflect. I am not sure - yes, I am. I distinctly remember having seen him run obliquely to the left there. It was just after I had lost my tent -- "

"Over that way?" asked Lige, pointing.

"Yes, that was the direction. I am positive of it now. But, if he went that way, he didn't follow you?" added the Professor hesitatingly.

"Do you know what lies there, less than ten rods away?" asked the guide, gravely.

"I don't understand you."

"There's a cliff there that drops down a clear hundred feet," answered Lige, impressively.

A heavy silence fell over the little group.

# CHAPTER VII

## OVER THE CLIFF

Professor Zepplin's face worked convulsively as he sought to control his emotions.

"You - you can't mean it, sir. You cannot mean that Walter has come to any real harm? I -- "

"I don't know. I'm only telling you what to expect."

"Then do something! Do something! For the love of manhood, do - " exploded the Professor, striding to the guide.

But Lige, having turned his back on the German tutor, was giving some brief directions to the boys, who were now fully dressed. They assented by vigorous nods, then promptly fell in behind him and held their torches close to the ground as if in search of something.

Reaching the bushes at the point where the Professor thought he had seen Walter Perkins disappear, they halted, the guide making a careful examination while the boys waited in silent expectancy.

Lige nodded reflectively.

"Yes; he went this way. You boys spread out, and if any of you observe even a broken twig that I have missed, let me know. The trail seems plain enough here."

And, the further he proceeded, the more convinced was Lige Thomas that his fears were soon to be fully realized.

Suddenly he paused, dropping onto his knees, in which position he cautiously crawled forward a few paces.

"Huh!" grunted the guide.

The boys, realizing that he had made some sort of a discovery, started forward with one accord.

"Stop!" commanded their guide sternly. "Don't you know you are standing on the very edge of the jumping-off place? Get down and crawl up by me here, Master Ned. But, be very careful. Leave your torch."

Ned quickly obeyed the instructions of the guide, lying down flat on his stomach, and wriggling along in that way as best he could.

Lige took a firm hold of his belt.

"I can't see anything," breathed the boy.

At first his eyes were unable to pierce the blackness. But after a little, as they became more accustomed to it, he began to comprehend. Below him yawned a black, forbidding chasm.

Ned shivered.

"Walt didn't - didn't -- "

Lige inclined his head.

"Are you going to keep me in this suspense all night?" demanded the Professor irritably. "What have you discovered?"

The guide, before replying, assisted Ned back to his feet, leading him to a safe distance beyoud the dangerous precipice.

"There's no doubt of it at all, Professor. He has left a trail as plain as a cougar's in winter. He must have stepped off the edge at the exact point where you saw me lying."

"Then - then you think - you believe -- "

"That he has been dashed to his death on the rocks a hundred feet below," added Lige solemnly. "Nothing short of a miracle could have saved him, and miracles ain't common in the Rockies."

The boys gazed into each other's eyes, then turned away. None dared trust his voice to speak. It was some moments before the Professor had succeeded in exercising enough self-control to use his own.

"Wh - what can we do?" he asked hoarsely.

"Nothing, except go down and pick him up -- "

"But how?"

"By going back a mile we shall hit a trail that will lead

us down into the gulch. But we'll have to leave the ponies and go down on foot. Not being experienced, I'm afraid to trust them. Only the most sure-footed ponies could pick their way where one misstep would send them to the bottom."

Returning to camp, and piling the fire high with fresh wood, the boys secured the ponies, and, led by Lige, struck off over the hack trail. It was a silent group of sad-faced boys that followed the mountain guide, and not a syllable was spoken, save now and then a word of direction from Lige, uttered in a low voice.

After somewhat more than half an hour's rough groping over rocks, through tangled underbrush and miniature gorges, Lige called a halt while he took careful account of their surroundings. His eye for a trail was unerring, and he was able to read at a glance the lesson it taught.

"Here is where we turn off," he announced. "Follow me in single file. But everybody keep close to the rocks at your right hand, and don't try to look down. I'm going to light a torch now."

The guide had had the forethought to bring a bundle of dry sticks, some of which he now proceeded to light, and, holding the torch high above his head, that the light might not flare directly in their eyes, he began the descent, followed cautiously by the others of the party. Yet, so filled were the minds of the boys with their new sorrow that they gave little heed to the perils that lay about them.

At last they came to the end of the long, dangerous descent, and, turning sharply to the right, picked their way through the cottonwood forest to the northwest.

Not a word had the Professor spoken since they left the camp, until observing a faint light in the sky some distance beyoud them, he asked the guide what it was.

"That's the light from our camp fire. "We are getting near the place," he answered shortly.

Professor Zepplin groaned.

Now, realizing the necessity for more light, Lige procured an armful of dry, dead limbs, all of which he bound into torches, and, lighting them, passed them to the others. With the aid of these the rocks all about them were thrown up into hold relief.

The boys were spread out in open order and directed to keep their eyes on the ground, remaining fully a dozen paces behind their leader, who of course, was the guide himself.

Peering here and there, starting at every flickering shadow, their nerves keyed to a high pitch, they began the sad task of searching for the body of their young companion.

Finally they reached the point which Lige knew to be almost directly beneath the spot where Walter was supposed to have stepped off into space.

"Remain where you are, please," ordered the guide.

Continuing in the direction which he had been following for several rods, Lige turned and made a sweeping detour, fanning the ground with his torch, as he picked his way carefully along.

"Wh - wha - what do you find?" breathed the Professor as Lige turned and came back to them.

"Nothing."

"Nothing? What does that mean?"

"That the boy's not here. That's all."

"Not - here!" marveled the three lads, and even that was a distinct relief to them. If Walter had not been dashed to death on the rocks at the bottom of the gulch, then there still was hope that he might be alive. However, this faint hope was shattered by Lige Thomas's next remark.

"The body may have caught on a root somewhere up the mountain side, "he added." I am afraid we shall have to go back and wait for daylight. But we'll see what can be done. I don't want to give it up until I am sure."

"Sure of what?" asked the Professor.

"That the boy is dead. Look!" exclaimed the guide, fairly diving to the ground, and rising with a round stone in his hand. He held it up almost triumphantly for their inspection.

But his find failed to make any noticeable impression upon either the boys or Professor Zepplin. They knew that in some mysterious way it must be connected with the loss of their companion, though just how they were at a loss to understand.

"I don't catch your idea, Lige," stammered the Professor. "I understand that you have picked up a stone. What has that to do with Walter?"

"Why, don't you see? He must have dislodged it when he fell off the mountain."

"No; I do not see why you say that."

"And up there, if you will look sharply, you will observe the path it followed coming down," continued Lige, elevating the torch that they might judge for themselves of the correctness of his assertion.

But, keen-eyed as were most of the party, they were unable to find the tell-tale marks which were so plain to the mountaineer.

"What do you think we had better do, sir?" asked Tad Butler anxiously.

"Go back to camp. I should like to leave someone here - but -- "

"I'll stay, if you wish," offered Tad promptly.

"No, I couldn't think of it. It's too risky, There is no need of our getting into more trouble. If you knew the mountains better it might be different. If I left you here you might get into more difficulties, even, than your friend has. No; we'll go back together. It is doubtful if we could do anything for poor Master Walter now. No human being could go over that cliff and still be alive. A bob-cat might do it, but not a man or a boy," announced the guide, with a note of finality in his tone.

Sorrowfully the party turned and began to retrace their steps. But the necessity for caution not being so great on the return, most of the way being up a steep declivity, they moved along much faster than had been the case on their previous journey over the trail.

The return to camp was accomplished without incident, and the boys slipped away to their tents that they might be alone with their thoughts.

Professor Zepplin and the guide, however, sat down by the camp fire, where they talked in low tones.

Tad, upon reaching his tent, threw himself on his cot, burying his head in his arms.

"I can't stand it! I simply can't!" he exclaimed after a little. "It's too awful!"

The boy sprang up, and going outside, paced restlessly back and forth in front of the tent, with hands thrust deep into his trousers pockets, manfully struggling to keep hack the tears that persistently came into his eyes.

A sudden thought occurred to him.

With a quick, inquiring glance at the two figures by the fire, Tad slipped quietly to the left, and nearing the scene of the accident, crept cautiously along on all fours. He flattened himself on the ground, face down, his head at the very spot where his companion had, supposedly, taken the fatal plunge.

For several minutes the boy lay there, now and then his slight figure shaken by a sob that he was powerless to keep back.

Frank Gee Patchin

"I cannot have it - I don't believe it is true. I wish it had been I instead of Walt," he muttered in the excess of his grief. "I -- "

Tad cheeked himself sharply and raised his head.

"I thought I heard something," he breathed. "I know I heard something."

He listened intently and shivered.

Yet the only sounds that broke the stillness of the mountain night were the faint calls of the night birds and the distant cry of a roaming cougar.

"H-e-l-p!"

Faint though the call was, it smote Tad Butler's ears like a blow. Never had the sound of a human voice thrilled him as did that plaintive appeal from the black depths below.

He hesitated, to make sure that it was not a delusion of his excited imagination.

Once more the call came.

"Help!"

This time, however, it was uttered in the shrill, piercing voice of Tad Butler himself, and the men back there by the camp fire started to their feet in sudden alarm while Ned Rector and Stacy Brown came tumbling from their tents in terrified haste.

"What is it! What is it?" they shouted.

Instead of answering them, Lige Thomas, with a mighty leap, cleared the circle of light and sprang for the bushes from which the sound had seemed to come. He was followed quickly by the others. Both the guide and Professor Zepplin had recognized the voice, and each believed that Tad Butler had gone to share the fate of Walter Perkins.

Yet, when Lige heard Tad tearing through the underbrush toward him, he knew that this was not the case.

"What is it?" bellowed the guide in a strident voice.

"It's Walt! He's down there! Quick! Help!"

# CHAPTER VIII

## A DARING RESCUE

Lige thrust the excited boy to one side. Running to the edge of the cliff, he leaned over and listened intently.

A moment more and he too caught the plaintive cry for help from below.

It was the first time thus far on the journey that Lige Thomas had
manifested the slightest sign of excitement. Just now, however, there
could be no doubt at all that he was intensely agitated.

"Keep back! Keep back!" he shouted, as the boys and Professor Zepplin began crowding near the masked edge of the cliff. "You'll all be over if you don't have a care. We've got trouble enough on our hands without having the rest of you jump into it."

"What is it?" demanded the Professor breathlessly.

"It's Master Walt," snapped the guide. "Stand still. Don't move an inch. I'm going back for a torch," he commanded, leaping by them on his way to the camp fire.

"Where - is - he?" stammered the Professor, not observing that the guide had left them.

"Down there, sir," explained Tad, pointing to the ledge of rock over which Walter had fallen.

"I know - I know - but -- "

"I heard him call. Walt's alive! Walt's alive! But I don't know how we are going to get him."

The shout of joy that had framed itself on the lips of Ned Rector and Stacy Brown died out in an indistinct murmur.

"Is it possible! What are we going to do, Thomas - how are we to rescue the boy?"

Lige Thomas made no reply to the question as he ran past them, and, dropping down, leaned over the cliff, holding the torch he had brought far out ahead of him.

"See anything?" asked Tad tremulously, creeping to his side.

"Looks like a clump of bushes down there. But I ain't sure. Can you make it out?"

"No. All I can see is rocks and shadows. Where is it that you think you see bushes?"

"Over there to the right, just near the edge of the light space made by the torch light," answered the guide.

"Yes," agreed Tad, "that does look like bushes. I'll call to Walter and tell him we are coming. Hey, Walter!

Where are you?" "H - e - r - e," was the faint response. "All right, old man. Stick tight and don't get scared. We'll have you out of that in no time."

"Don't move around. Lie perfectly still," warned the guide. "Are you hurt?"

To this question Walter made some reply that was unintelligible to them.

"Now, what are we going to do, I'd like to know?" asked Ned.

"I don't know," answered Lige, frowning thoughtfully. "It's a tough job. If I had a couple of mountaineers who knew their business, we'd stand a better chance of pulling him up."

"Why not get a rope and let it down to him," suggested Tad.

"Yes, that's the only way we can do it. Run over to the cook tent and tell Jose to give you those rawhide lariats that he will find behind his bunk. Hurry!"

Tad was off almost before the words were out of the mouth of the guide, and in the briefest possible time came racing back with the leather coils, which he tossed to Lige before reaching him, that there might not be even a second's delay.

The mountaineer quickly formed a loop in one end of the rope, making it large enough to permit of its slipping over the shoulders of a man. This he dropped over the brink, after splicing two lariats together, and directing Ned Rector to make the other end fast about the trunk of a tree by giving it a couple of hitches.

"Hello, down there! Let me know when the rope reaches you. Can you slip it over your shoulders and under your arms?" called the guide.

There was no response.

"I say, down there!" shouted Lige.

"That's funny," wondered Tad. "H-e-l-l-o-o-o-o, Walt!"

But not a sound came up from the black depths in answer to the boy's hail. They gazed at each other in perplexity.

"Has - he - gone?" asked the Professor weakly.

"No. We should have heard him if he had," answered Lige. "If I could see him I'd lasso him and haul him up. But I don't dare try it. Then again, these roots on a wall of rock ain't any too strong usually. I don't dare try any experiments."

"What do you think has happened to him?" asked Tad in a troubled voice.

"Fainted, probably. He ain't very strong, you know. And that tumble's enough to knock the sense out of a full grown man. Ain't no use to expect him to hook himself onto the line, even if he does wake up," decided the guide with emphasis, beginning to haul up the lariat, which he coiled neatly on the rock in front of him.

"Then what are we going to do? We've got to get Walt

up here, even if I have to jump over after him," said Tad firmly.

"Right you are, young man. But talking won't do it. Something else besides saying you're going to will be necessary."

"What would you suggest!"

"One of us must go down there," was the guide's startling announcement. "That's the only way we can reach him," explained Lige, dangling the loop of the lariat in his hands as he looked from one to the other.

"D - do - down in that dark place? Oh!" exclaimed Chunky.

"In that case, you will have to go yourself, Thomas," decided the Professor sharply. "I could not think of allowing any of my charges to take so terrible a risk, and -- "

"Let me go, Mr. Thomas," interrupted Ned Rector, stepping forward, with almost a challenge in his eyes.

"No; I am the lighter of the two," urged Tad. "I am the one to go after Walt, if anyone has to. I'll go down, Mr. Thomas."

"Master Tad is right," decided the guide, gazing at the two boys approvingly. "It will be better for him to go, if he will -- "

"And he most certainly will," interrupted Tad, advancing a step.

"I protest!" shouted the Professor. "You yourself should go, Lige. You are -- "

"I am needed right here, sir," replied the guide, shortly. "You'd have both of us at the bottom if I left it to you to take care of this end."

"I'm ready, sir when you are," reminded Tad.

The guide, without further delay, and giving no heed to Professor Zepplin's nervous protests, slipped the noose over Tad's shoulders, and, drawing it down and up under his arms, secured the knot so that the loop might not tighten under the weight of the boy's body.

"Now, be very careful. Make no sudden moves. And, if you meet with anything unlooked for, let me know at once. You know, you will have to stay down there while we are drawing the boy up. But, before removing the rope from your own body, make sure that you are safe. If you find the support too weak to bear your weight, let me know. I'll send down another rope to which you can tie yourself until we get Master Walter to the top. Be sure to fasten him securely to the loop before you give the signal to haul up," warned the guide. "Here, put my gun in your pocket."

"I understand." "Are you ready?"

"Yes."

Tad tossed away his sombrero and sat down on a shelf of rock at the edge of the cliff, his feet dangling over.

The lad's face was pale, the lines on it standing out in sharp ridges; but not by so much as the flicker of an eyelid did he betray the slightest nervousness. Yet Tad Butler realized fully the perilous nature of his undertaking, and that the least mistake on his part or on the part of those above him might mean a sudden end to his earthlyambitions.

Lige shortened the hitch about the tree, until the line drew taut. After winding the end tightly about his own arm, he handed a lighted torch to Tad.

It was a trying moment for all of them, and naturally more so for the boy who was about to descend into the unknown depths of the mountain canyou.

"Right!" announced the guide in a reassuring voice.

Tad made no reply, but, turning so that he faced them, let himself carefully over the ledge, his right hand holding the torch, his left firmly gripping the ledge so that there might be no jolt on the line by a too sudden stepping-off.

"Good!" approved Lige encouragingly, beginning to let the rawhide slip slowly around the trunk of the tree. As he did so, Tad felt himself gradually sinking into the sombre depths.

He tilted his head to look up. The movement sent his body swaying giddily from side to side.

Cautiously placing a hand against the rocks to steady himself, Tad wisely concluded that hereafter it would not pay to be too curious.

"Hold a torch over the edge of the cliff, Master Ned," directed the guide. "Better lie down so you, too, don't take a notion to fall off. Keep your eyes shut till I tell you to open them."

Slowly, but steadily, the slender line was paid out, amid a tense silence on the part of the little group at the top of the can you. After what seemed to them hours, a sharp call from the depths reached their ears.

Lige quickly made fast the line to a tree.

"Yes? Got him?" he answered, leaning over the cliff.

"I see him," called Tad, his voice sounding hollow and unnatural to those above. "He's so far to the right of me that I can't reach him. Will it be all right for me to swing myself?"

"Where is he?"

"Lodged in the branches of a pinyon tree, I think it is. But he doesn't answer me."

"Wait a minute," cautioned the mountaineer.

Lige searched until he found a limb some three inches in diameter, and this he placed under the rope so as to relieve the strain of the rock upon it, that there might be no danger of the leather being sawed in two by contact with the ledge.

"All right. Now try it."

The creaking of the rawhide told them that Tad Butler was swaying from side to side, fifty feet below them, at the end of a slender line. Lige, leaning over the brink, was able to follow the boy's movements by the aid of the thin arc of light made by the torch in Tad's hand.

At last, the thread of light contracted into a point, and the watching guide knew that the courageous boy had finally reached the pinyon tree.

Then followed a long period of suspense. But from the cautious movements of the light far below them, the guide understood that the lad was at work carrying out his part of the task of rescue to the best of his ability.

"Why doesn't he say something?" cried the Professor, unable to restrain his impatience longer, bis over-wrought nerves almost at the breaking point.

"Keep still! Don't bother him. The boy's doing the best he can. Mebby you think he's having some sort of a picnic down there, eh?" glared Lige.

"A - l - l right!"

Tad's voice, now strong and clear, rose from the depths of the canyou.

"Shall we haul up?" asked Lige, making a megaphone of his hands.

"Yes; haul away. Tell them Walt's all right. He can talk now," was the answer that carried with it such a note of gladness that Ned and Stacy were unable to resist a shout of joy.

"Lend a hand here," commanded Lige, taking firm hold of the line, and stepping to the edge that he might command both ends of the operation. "Are you all safe down there, Tad?"

"Sure thing!" answered the boy.

Very slowly, restraining their inclination to haul the rope in with all speed only because the warning eyes of the guide were upon them, the two boys, assisted by Professor Zepplin, began hoisting Walter Perkins toward the top.

In a few moments the sinewy hands of the guide gripped Walter by an arm and dragged him safely to the table rock.

Walter had fully regained consciousness by this time, and a brief examination showed that he had sustained no serious injury, he having struck on the yielding branches of the pinyon, which broke his fall and saved his life. Beyond sundry bruises, a black eye and a thin crimson line on the right cheek where a branch had raked it, Walter Perkins was practically unharmed after his perilous experience.

But it was a trying moment for Tad Butler, down there alone in the branches of the pinyon tree, with fifty feet of nothingness beneath him and a sheer wall that extended an equal distance above him.

Nor was his sense of security increased when, in shifting his position, the torch fell from his grasp, the fagots scattering as they slipped down between the limbs of the tree and whirling in ever-diminishing circles until finally he heard them clatter on the rocks below.

The  boy could not repress a shudder. Closing his eyes,

he clung to the slender support with grim courage until a hail from above told him that the rawhide loop was rapidly squirming down toward him.

This time Lige had allowed for his mistaken reckoning when Tad had first descended, and the boy grasped eagerly at the leather as he felt it gently slap against his cheek.

A few moments more, and he, too, had been hauled safely to the top, amid the wild cheers of his companions and the congratulations of the guide and Professor Zepplin.

# CHAPTER IX

## RIFLES AND PONIES

After having been well rubbed down by the guide, and given a steaming cup of tea, Walter was put to bed, protesting stubbornly that he was all right and that their attentions were unnecessary.

But Lige Thomas was firm.

"You'll be that lame, to-morrow, you can't reach a stirrup. I want you to be fit, for we have a long journey ahead of us."

Walter soon fell into a deep sleep, while Tad and Ned, too full of the events of the night to go to sleep at once, sat by the camp fire discussing the stirring scenes through which they had so recently passed, until the deep, rhythmic snores of Stacy Brown reminded them that they, too, should seek their pine bough cots if they intended to get any more rest that night.

Next morning the camp slept late in spite of itself - that is, all save Lige Thomas. He was up with the sun, busying himself with getting the outfit ready for a prompt start.

At nine o'clock the guide routed them out, and the

boys, after washing themselves in the cool, refreshing waters of a little mountain stream, announced themselves as ready to eat anything that might be placed before them.

Walter, still pale from his recent experience, but smiling happily, took his place with the rest and ate as heartily as they did of the crisp bacon that Jose had prepared.

"Now that you young gentleman are all together, it's a good time to give you some advice," said Lige.

"Guess I'm the one who needs it most," laughed Walter.

"He's had his already," chuckled Chunky Brown.

"But yours is still coming to you," added Ned maliciously.

"You must keep in mind that these mountains are full of danger," continued the guide. "Even an experienced mountaineer sometimes goes wrong, losing his life as the result. So, before any one of you takes a step, be sure that your foot is going to land on something solid. As we get up into the Park Range you will find the country rougher, and still more caution will be necessary. But you're going to be all right. You boys have the right sort of stuff in you. Not many fellows of Master Tad's age would have had the courage to do what he did last night."

Tad Butler flushed a rosy red, and devoted his attention to his bacon.

"Yes, he saved my life," breathed Walter. "You all did your share too."

"There's one thing I should like to do more than anything else," interrupted Ned, changing the subject.

"And that?" inquired the Professor.

"To shoot a bear."

"Wow!" exclaimed Chunky.

"And so should I," agreed Tad, his blue eyes opening wide. "The biggest thing I ever shot was a woodchuck."

"You will have a chance to do some hunting soon," replied the guide. "We shall be on the hunting grounds in a day or so, if we have good luck, and none of you falls off a mountain. Then I am going to show you some real sport."

"Oh, that will be fine," chorused the boys.

"I believe I should like to try my hand at it, too," added the Professor. "Do you know, young gentlemen, I have not been on a hunting trip since I hunted wild boar in the Black Forest with General von Moltke! You may talk about the savagery of your native bear. But, for real brutality, I recommend the wild boar."

"Yes, but wait a minute," objected Ned Rector, his face sobering. "How are we going to hunt? We have no guns to hunt with. Mr. Thomas has the only rifle in the party."

"That's so," agreed Tad. "I hadn't thought of that. I should have brought my old rifle with me."

The guide smiled good-naturedly and motioned to Jose.

"Do you know where that long package marked 'hard tack' is, Jose?" he asked.

The cook said he did.

"Bring it to me," directed Lige so low that the others did not catch his words.

The package was placed on the ground at Lige's side a moment later.

"What is it?" asked Chunky, stretching his neck so he could look over the table.

"Your curiosity will be the death of you some day if you don't correct the habit," warned Ned. "If you'll use your eyes you will observe that the package contains hard tack, and -- "

However, something in the shape of the four wrapped objects taken from the bundle, and laid on the ground, did not exactly correspond with their idea of what hard tack looked like.

The boys rose full of curiosity.

"Wha - what -- " gasped Ned.

"It's - guns!" fairly shouted Tad Butler.

Sure enough, it was.

Undoing the other three packages, the guide laid before their astonished eyes four handsome thirty-eight calibre repeating rifles.

The boys looked at each other questioningly.

At first they could scarcely believe it to be true.

"Are - are they for us - for us to use?" stammered Tad.

"That's what they're for, young gentlemen," smiled the guide. "You surely didn't expect to go hunting without guns, did you? At the Professor's suggestion I have been keeping them as a sort of surprise for you."

"Three cheers for Lige Thomas and Professor Zepplin," cried Ned Rector, in which the boys joined with a will, their shouts echoing back to them from the rocky peaks on the other side of the gulch.

"Rifles and ponies! We surely ought to be happy!" laughed Tad, with flashing eyes. "Any boy with those two things wouldn't change places with a king, would he, fellows?"

"No!" answered the Pony Riders at the top of their voices. "Not even for a whole monarchy!"

Lige was beset by a perfect clamor of questions as to when they were to have a chance to try the guns on real game.

"One at a time - one at a time," begged the guide. "First I must find out how well you boys can shoot.

Has any of you ever handled a gun before?"

"I have," spoke up Tad promptly.

"And I," added Ned Rector.

"I've done a little shooting with my thirty-two calibre," said Walter. "But I don't call myself much of a shot."

"And how about you, Master Stacy?" smiled the guide.

"I? Why, I can shoot a bull's eye with a how and arrow. But somehow, when I try to fire a real gun, I can't help shutting my eyes before the thing goes off."

"That's bad."

"Then I don't hit anything - that is, not the thing I want to hit," he added humorously, at which there was a loud laugh from the other boys.

"Won't do at all," decided the guide with a shake of the head. "You will have to learn to do better than that before we take you out."

"Yes, he'll have to before I go gunning with him," growled Ned Rector. "Any man who shuts his eyes when he's getting ready to shoot, is no friend of mine, especially if I happen to be in the neighborhood."

"Yes," agreed Lige. "We'll have to go out for a little practice - this morning if you wish. I guess we can spare the time. But we must not waste too much of it, as we have an eighteen mile journey ahead of us over a rough trail, and I want to reach Bald Mountain before night.

To-morrow will be Sunday, and we must have a nice camping place, as you will want to rest and get ready for the busy week ahead of us. At any rate, you boys can try out the guns this morning and get the sights regulated. Jose bring me a box of those thirty-eights, will you?"

Wistful glances were cast at the pasteboard box, as the boys fondled the guns, worked the cartridge ejectors, examined the magazines and looked over the sights at imaginary game.

"Better fall to, now, and strike camp, so the pack train can go on ahead," advised the guide. "When we finish shooting you can strap your guns to the saddles, or carry them over your backs, as you prefer. You see they have a leather on them for the purpose."

There were no doubts in the minds of the Pony Riders as to how they would carry the weapons. As they set about obeying the instructions of the guide, they pictured themselves riding over the mountains like a troop of cavalry, rifles hanging across their backs, following the trail of a band of real Indians.

The camp was struck in record time that morning, and the tents, neatly rolled, soon were strapped to the backs of the sleepy burros. Jose attended to the packing of the commissary.

"I think we are ready, Mr. Thomas," announced Tad, their task having been completed.

The boys shouldered their guns proudly.

"Oh, yes; there is something else that goes with it,"

advised Lige, after glancing critically over the boys and their outfits." I had almost forgotten it. Fine general I'd make in war time!"

The guide ran to the cook tent which Jose was packing, returning in a moment with another of those mysterious packages.

By now the Pony Riders were worked up to a high pitch of excitement and anticipation.

"What have you got?" asked Chunky, with his usual curiosity.

"I'll show you if you'll wait a minute," whereupon the guide opened the package, holding the contents toward them.

"What is it!" marveled Chunky, eyeing the things gingerly.

"I know! Cartridge belts!" shouted Ned Rector.

And cartridge belts they were - regulation canvas belts, each with a shining brass buckle, bearing a spread eagle on its face, the belts each having compartments for forty-five rounds of ammunition.

Once more the Pony Riders made the mountains ring with their shouts of joy in which not even the dignified German Professor could resist joining.

Stacy Brown in the meantime, had been greedily filling his belt with the cartridges, until finally there was room for no more.

The other three boys, who had quickly strapped on their belts, were parading about with guns on their shoulders, Walter Perkins giving them their orders.

"Wow! But this thing is heavy," exclaimed Chunky, the weight of his loaded belt tugging at his waist line.

"Here, here, Master Brown! You don't need all those shells. Put all but ten of them back in the box," laughed the guide,

"They're not good to eat, Chunky," advised Walter.

"Huh!" grunted Ned Rector. "Anybody would think he was going into battle. Why, a soldier doesn't carry any more bullets than that. And what's more, Mr. Chunky Brown, if you intend to shoot off a belt full of those shells, it's me for a rocky cave where the bullets can't reach. Eh, Tad?"

Tad nodded and grinned.

"I'm with you in that."

"We all have precious lives to save," added Ned.

"We are all ready," announced the guide. "Jose, you bear to the right after you leave camp and follow the blazed trail. We shall take the lower trail. Push right along so as to have a meal ready for us when we get in. We'll be hungry by that time."

"Have we any lunch with us?" asked the Professor.

"Yes, in the saddle bags."

A few moments later the boys were waking the echoes with the crashing explosions of their weapons as they banged away at the targets.

# CHAPTER X

## THE LOSS OF THE PACK TRAIN

"Feels good to be in the saddle again, doesn't it, Walt?"

"Yes, Ned. At least it's better than falling over a cliff. How do you feel, Chunky?"

"Shoulder aches where the gun kicked me. I didn't think a gun could hit so hard from both ends at the same time."

Stacy Brown worked his right arm up and down like a pump-handle, making a wry face as he did so.

The boys had completed their first target practice, in which Tad and Ned had carried off even honors, with Walter Perkins a close second, while Stacy Brown had hit pretty much everything within range except the target itself.

About the best they had been able to do with him was to induce him to keep his eyes open, at least, until the first finger of his right hand had begun to exert a gentle pressure on the trigger. Then, he would pinch his eyelids so tightly together as to compress his forehead into a series of small ridges.

Their practice had lasted some two hours, and now they were once more picking their way over the rough mountain trail, headed for Bald Mountain, and discussing the happenings of the night and morning.

Considerable amusement was afforded them when, on the journey, old Bobtail, as they had named the Professor's cob, stumbled and threw its rider over its head.

Fortunately, Professor Zepplin was not injured. He explained that he had had too many similar disasters while an officer in the German army, and that he did not mind a slight mishap like that at all. He declared that it reminded him so much of his younger days that he really enjoyed the sensation of falling off.

This caused the Pony Riders to shout with laughter, and Ned confided to Tad, by whose side he was riding, that he never knew the Professor was such a real sport.

From then on the afternoon passed quickly. Although the sun was shining brightly, the air was cool and invigorating, and a gentle breeze fanned their cheeks when the riders reached the higher places.

At such times the boys would break into exclamations of wonder at the gorgeous panorama which unfolded itself before them.

"Makes a fellow feel as if he were walking on air, doesn't it?" bubbled Stacy Brown.

"You will be in a minute, if you don't watch out where you are going," warned Ned, observing that the boy had unconsciously pulled his horse too near the outer edge of the trail." Walt tried that last night, and you know what happened to him."

"Yes, but Chunky would not come out of it quite so well," spoke up Tad.

"I reckon he'd break a rock or two on the way down," grinned Ned Rector, clucking to his pony.

About four o'clock that afternoon Lige announced that they had arrived at their destination. Yet not a sign of Jose and the pack train could they find. He had not arrived.

The faces of the Pony Riders grew long at this, for the ride had given them an appetite that would not bear trifling with.

"What do you suppose has happened to the pack train, Mr. Thomas?" asked Tad.

"Probably been delayed by a pack slipping off. But don't you worry. Jose will be along in good time," smiled Lige.

However, in his own mind the guide believed that, while this might be possible, it was more likely that the cook had missed his way, and was now wandering about the mountains. It was too late to go in search of the missing outfit that day, so there was nothing to do but to wait until morning, then to start out after it, in case the straggler had not come in by then.

Lige told the boys to stake down their live stock and make themselves at home while he went out for an observation. In the meantime the boys also took the opportunity to look about them.

Their new location they found to be a sightly one. The wild and rugged reaches of the Rockies stretched away at their feet as far as the eye could see, the hills and low mountains rising in sheer slopes, broken by cliffs and riven by deeply cut and gloomy gorges.

The Pony Riders gazed upon the scene in awe - at least three of them did.

"Splendid, is it not?" breathed Tad, his eyes growing large with wonder.

"Oh, I don't know. It isn't so much," replied Chunky lightly. "I've seen better. We've got bigger mountains in Massachusetts."

"Humph!" grunted Ned Rector, resuming his study of the scene, its beauties intensified by the colors in which the low-lying sun had bathed them.

A shot sounded off somewhere in front of and below them.

"What's that?" exclaimed Chunky, now aroused to sudden interest.

No one was able to answer him.

Soon two more shots followed, and Chunky; was sure that he heard a bullet sing by his head.

Professor Zepplin laughed, saying it was no doubt some one hunting, and that what the boy had imagined was a bullet was merely an echo.

"You no doubt will hear many shots while you are in the mountains. This is a place where people make a business of shooting, and even yourselves will be doing some of it within a few days, if all goes well. Perhaps the shot you heard was from Lige, trying his skill on some bird or animal."

When Lige returned, some little time after, the boys did not observe that he left his rifle in the bushes at the edge of the camp.

"Was that you shooting just now?" asked Tad.

Instead of answering the question, however, the guide called the boys to him.

"I'm going to teach you how to make beds in the mountains," he said. "We have not tried to make any like them yet -- "

"Beds? I don't see any beds to make," objected Chunky. "Where are they?"

"Get your hatchets and I'll show you," grinned Lige. "We have to discover a good many things when we are roughing it, you know."

Fetching their hatchets from the saddle bags, the boys cut great armfuls of pine boughs, all hands making two trips to camp and back in order to carry enough for the purpose. But, even then, they were mystified as to exactly what Thomas intended to do or how he would go about it to make a bed out of the stuff they had gathered.

Professor Zepplin watched the preparations with

interest, finding much that was new to him in the resourceful operations of the mountain guide.

Having heaped up a great pile of fragrant green stuff, Lige looked about him to fix upon the best locations for the beds he was about to make.

"Oh, I know," exclaimed Ned. "You are going to lay the stuff into piles so we can sleep on them."

"Not quite," grinned Lige." Watch me."

Carefully selecting the branches that he wanted, he stuck one after another of them into the ground, stem down, until he had outlined a fairly good bed. This done, he continued setting more of the green limbs, pushing each firmly into the ground until the mass became so thick and matted that it resembled a green hedge.

"There," he announced. "One bed is ready for you."

"Call that a bed?" sniffed Stacy. "Why, that wouldn't hold a baby. He'd fall through the slats."

"Try it. Lie down on it," smiled Lige.

Chunky did so, gingerly, then little by little a sheepish smile crept over his countenance.

"Why, it does hold me up."

"Of course it does."

"Say, fellows, this is great. It's softer than any feather bed I ever slept in. But it wouldn't be half so funny if a fellow made a mistake and got a branch off a thorn bush; would it, now?"

One after the other, the boys took turns in trying the new bed, and each was enthusiastic over it.

"I'll never sleep on any other kind as long as I live," decided Ned. "I'll have a tent in the back yard and a pine bed under it. What do you say, fellows?"

"I have an idea," smiled the Professor, "that you will get all you want of the experience this summer. Some other trips have been planned for you, and you no doubt will spend many nights in the open air before you return to your homes this fall. I'll say no more on the subject at present."

And Professor Zepplin steadfastly stuck to his word, leaving to their youthful imaginations the solution of the problem that he had presented.

"Get busy for firewood," called Lige.

"Why, it's almost dark," exclaimed Ned. "Where is that pack train? What are we going to do, Professor?"

"Ask the guide. He knows everything. He's the original wizard," laughed the German. "What do you think about it, Lige?"

"I might as well tell you all now - the pack train undoubtedly is lost in the mountains. We probably shall see nothing of Jose nor the pack train until some time to-morrow."

"Yes; but what are we going to do?" demanded Walter.

"Here we are, without a thing to eat, or a place to sleep."

"We have the pine beds," answered Tad. "That's a place to sleep, anyway."

"But we can't eat the beds," jeered Chunky.

"If you young gentlemen will build a fire, I'll see what I can do about getting you some supper," advised Lige." You know, we have to get used to difficulties in the mountains. In a short time you should be well able to take care of yourselves without any of my help."

Lige disappeared in the bushes, returning a few moments later, carrying a brace of some sort of animal by the hind legs.

"What's that?" demanded Stacy Brown, his eyes growing large.

"Jack-rabbits," answered the guide. "There are two of them. I shot them, and now we'll eat them. I was providing a supper for you when you heard those shots."

The boys set up a cheer. Now that the wholesome air of the mountains had in reality taken possession of their beings, they found themselves able to arouse enthusiasm over almost any subject.

Lige skilfully skinned the rabbits and dressed them. By the time he had accomplished this the fire was burning high, and out of it he scraped a bed of red hot coals, about which he built an oven of stones.

"Get two sharp sticks," he directed.

On these he spit the rabbits, thrusting them over the coals to cook, while the boys looked on wonderingly.

"You see," said the Professor, "it is possible for a man to find sustenance in almost any place - that is, if he knows how."

"I'd starve to death if I were turned loose up here," said Chunky.

"Of course you would; and I probably should share the same fate. The only mountain subject with which I am familiar is geology," said the Professor.

"And you can't eat rocks," grinned Ned.

"Just so."

"Now, boys, if you will go to my saddle bags you will find salt and pepper and some hard tack. Bring it all over here, fill your folding cups with water, and then I think we'll be ready for supper," announced the guide, after the rabbits had been done to a rich brown.

"Pardon me, sir, but I'm curious to know what we're going to do for plates, knives and forks," asked Tad.

"Do?

"Why, my young friend, we shall do without them. If you'll watch me carefully you will learn how."

By Lige's direction, the boys squatted down about a flat rock, after which the guide proceeded to carve the rabbits with his hunting-knife, seasoning the pieces with salt and pepper, yet doing all with tantalizing deliberation.

The boys looked on expectantly.

"Much as I need money, I wouldn't take four dollars and a half for my appetite at this very moment," declared Ned Rector, earnestly.

"It can't beat mine, fellows," laughed Walter. "I tell you, there's nothing like falling off a mountain to give a chap a full-grown hankering for real food."

"I should imagine it would shake one down a bit," agreed Tad. "What do you think about it, Chunky?"

But Chunky's reply was not clear to them, for the greater part of his face was buried in a flank of jack-rabbit, and he was able to talk with his eyes alone, which at that moment were large and expressive.

Never had a meal seemed to taste so good to these boys as did this crude repast, served on a rock several thousand feet in the air and with only such conveniences for eating it as nature had provided. But good humor prevailed and everybody was happy.

Chunky at last paused from his labor long enough to go to the spring for a cup of water.

"While you are up you might fetch some for the rest of us," suggested Ned.

So Chunky gathered up the cups and plodded to the spring, chewing vigorously as he went. However, finding it inconvenient to carry all the cups at one time, he left his own at the spring, returning with those of the others, filled with cool, sparkling water.

The boys were profuse in their thanks, to which Stacy bowed with great ceremony and returned to the spring for more water.

For the moment, in the conversation that followed, they forgot Clunky entirely. But he was recalled sharply to their minds a few minutes later.

"Pussy, pussy, pussy!"

Ned and Tad turned inquiringly at the sound. Lige and the Professor, being engaged in earnest conversation at the time, had not heard Stacy Brown's plaintive call off behind the rocks youder.

The Pony Riders looked at each other and roared.

"Well, what do you think of that?" laughed Ned. "That kid has gone and picked up a cat. Who would ever think of finding a cat up here?"

"What's that?" demanded Lige sharply, turning to them.

"Why, Chunky's found a -- "

"Pussy, pussy, pussy! Nice pussy. Come here, pussy. That's a good kittie. Puss, puss, puss," continued the soothing voice of the boy.

Had Lige Thomas been projected from a huge bow-gun he probably would not have leaped forward with much greater quickness than he did in this instance, bowling over the Professor as he sprang by him, and making for the spring m mighty strides.

"Leave him alone!" he roared.

The guide had heard and understood. He was hurrying to the rescue.

Those by the camp fire heard two sharp, quick explosions from the guide's revolver, followed by a squall of rage and pain and a great floundering about in the bushes. Then the guide appeared around the corner of a large rock, leading Chunky by one ear, the latter taking as long strides as his short legs would permit, to relieve the strain on the aforesaid ear.

"Wha - what -- " stammered the Professor.

The boys had sprung to their feet in alarm at the crack of the pistol, and stood, amazement written on their faces, as Lige and Chunky came toward them.

"What's the row?" asked Ned Rector in as firm a voice as he could muster.

"I got a pussy and he tried to shoot it," wailed Chunky.

"Pussy! Huh! He got a bob-cat and he was trying to catch the brute, " growled the guide. "Lucky I got there when I did."

Stacy's eyes opened wide and his face blanched.

"A - a bob-cat?" they gasped.

"Yes; I put a shot into him, but it did not kill kill him! Hear him squall?" the guide made answer.

"Well of all the idiotic things I ever heard of!" exclaimed Ned, gazing at Chunky in bewilderment.

"Yes; it was all of that," grinned Lige.

# CHAPTER XI

## CHUNKY GETS THE CAT

Wake up, fellows! The sun is up!" shouted Tad Butler, as Sunday morning dawned bright and beautiful, the birds now making the mountains ring with their joyous songs.

The Pony Riders rose up, rubbing their eyes sleepily.

"What time is it?" asked Ned Rector.

"Half-past six."

"Too early to sing. I refuse to sit on a bough and sing at any such unearthly hour."

"Huh! I should say so," agreed Stacy Brown, turning over and burying his face in the fragrant green boughs of his cot.

Still, the boys had no patience with Chunky's dislike to early rising, even though they themselves were not averse to a morning cat-nap. With a yell, they tumbled from their cots, descending upon Chunky in a bunch, pulling him from his bed without regard to the way in which they did so. His ill-natured protests went for nothing.

"I wonder where the guide is?" asked Walter, after they had thoroughly awakened their companion.

"Probably gone gunning for our breakfast," answered Tad.

"I think he has gone after the pack train," said the Professor. "He told me last night that he should start at daybreak, and that you would find some rabbit and hard tack for your breakfast under a flat stone back of his cot. I am afraid you will have to be satisfied with a cold meal this morning, unless you think you want to build a fire and warm up the food."

"Of course we will. Lige Thomas needn't think he's the only one in the party who can get a meal out of nothing," answered Ned proudly, starting off to gather sticks for the fire.

But when they went to get the rabbit there was no rabbit. The stone under which it had been placed was there right enough, as were several chunks of hard tack. The stone, however, had been turned over and the meat was nowhere to be found.

"That settles it," said Ned ruefully. "I never had an appetite yet that it didn't meet with the disappointment of it's young life. Now, who do you suppose took that food!"

"Perhaps it was another of Chunky's pussy cats," laughed Walter.

"Don't we get anything to eat!" asked Stacy in a plaintive voice, glancing from one to the other of his companions.

"Yes, of course. You can go out in the bushes and browse, if you are hungry enough," suggested Ned. "As for myself I'm going to the spring and wash, and after that fill myself up on cold water. That may make my stomach forget, for a while, that it has a grievance."

"I'm going to bed," growled Stacy.

"You'll do nothing of the sort," shouted the boys, grabbing their roly-poly president and rushing him back and forth to wake him up again. "No Pony Rider is allowed to sleep after sun-up."

"Professor, I have a suggestion to make," said Tad, approaching Professor Zepplin, who was sitting on the edge of his cot, making a meal of a cup of water, seemingly well pleased that that much had been left to him.

"I'll hear it, sir."

"Will you let me go out with my rifle to look for some game for breakfast? Ned has three shells left in his belt. I think I shall be able to shoot something. There's no telling when Mr. Thomas will return with the pack."

"I couldn't think of it, my boy."

"I'll take care of myself, Professor."

"No. The responsibility is too great. We have had enough trouble already. I have not the least doubt that a resourceful young man like yourself could take care of himself under almost any conditions. But I do not dare take the risk. And, besides, a day's fast will do you all good. I remember when I was an officer in the German army -- "

"Professor, may we go out and follow the trail of Chunky's pussy cat?" interrupted Walter. "Ned has found the trail, and says he can follow it by the blood spots. Perhaps we'll find the animal dead near by, and the skin would be a fine trophy of our hunt in the Rockies."

"Certainly not. This is Sunday, young gentlemen, and even in the mountains we must preserve some sort of decorum on that day."

"Oh, very well," answered Walter politely, covering his disappointment with a smile.

"All days look alike to me up here," grunted Ned. "If it wasn't that one had a calendar he wouldn't even know when Sunday did come. Now, would he -- "

"I've got him! I've got him!" came the sudden and startling yell from the bushes, accompanied by a series of resounding whacks and a great threshing about in the thick undergrowth.

The boys paused, not realizing, at first, to whom the excited voice belonged.

"Come help me! I've got him!"

"Chunky!" they groaned. "He's at it again!"

Professor Zepplin leaped from his cot, striding off in the direction from which Stacy Brown's triumphant voice had come, and followed by the rest of the party on the run. All four of them crashed into the bushes at the same instant, shouting words of warning to Stacy.

They did not know what it all meant, but the boys were sure that he had gotten himself into some new danger.

Chunky had slipped away some moments before, after Ned Rector had discovered the trail of the bob-cat. His companions, however, had not missed him, so Stacy was free to follow his own inclinations.

"Where are you?" cried the Professor.

"Here! here!"

Whack! whack! came the sound from a rapidly wielded club again, accompanied by a vicious spitting and snarling that caused the boys to hesitate, for a brief second, in their mad dash for the underbrush.

As they emerged into a little open space, made so largely by the battle that was being waged there, their eyes fairly bulged with surprise.

There was Stacy Brown, hatless, his face red and perspiring, and in front of him a snarling bob-cat at bay.

They saw at once that the animal had been wounded, two of its legs apparently having been broken, while blood flowed freely from a wound in its side.

Chunky was prancing about in what appeared to be an imitation of an Indian war dance, now and again darting in and delivering a telling blow with the club held firmly in both hands, landing it on whatever part of the animal's anatomy he could most easily reach. The beast was snapping blindly at the weapon which Chunky was using with telling effect.

The boys in their surprise were unable to do more than stand and stare for the moment. That Chunky Brown had had the courage to attack a bob-cat, even though it already had been seriously wounded, passed all comprehension.

"Stop!" commanded the Professor, finding his voice at last.

Whack!

Stacy landed a blow fairly on the top of the brute's skull, causing the animal to sway dizzily.

Paying not the slightest heed to the Professor's stern command, the excited boy followed up his last successful blow by planting another in the same place.

But the savage little beast, though probably unable to see its enemies, was showing its yellow teeth and squalling in its deadly anger, the jaws coming together with a snap like that from the sudden springing of a steel trap.

"Stand back!" ordered the Professor. "Don't touch him! Get away, boys!"

They were obliged to grab Chunky by the arms, fairly dragging him from his victim, so filled was he with the fever of the chase and a resolve to conquer his savage little enemy.

Professor Zepplin, once they had gotten Chunky out of the way, stepped as near to the bob-cat as he deemed prudent. Drawing his heavy army revolver, he took careful aim, shooting the beast through the head.

The Pony Riders uttered a triumphant shout.

The Professor waved them back as they pressed forward, and planted another bullet in the animal's head to make sure that it was thoroughly finished.

"Hooray for the president of the Pony Riders!" shouted Ned Rector.

"Hip-hip hooray! T-i-g-e-r!" roared the boys, grabbing Chunky and tossing him back and forth, making of him a veritable medicine ball.

"What's the matter with Chunky?" cried Walter.

"Chunky's all right," chorused the band.

"Who's no tenderfoot?"

"Chunky's Brown's no tenderfoot."

Puffing out his cheeks, and squaring his shoulders, Stacy swaggered over to the dead bob-cat, violently pulling its ear.

"He tried to bite me," explained the boy. "See - he tore a lacer in my leggin. I didn't see him till I almost stepped on him. I knew right off that it was the pussy that Lige shot at last night."

"What happened then?" asked Tad, with an admiring

grin on his face.

"I fetched him one on the side of the head with a club. He jumped at me and I hit him again. About that time I called, and you fellows came up. But I got him, didn't I, Professor?"

"You did, my lad. But you took a great risk in attempting to do so," smiled the Professor, picking the dead animal up and hefting it. "I think he'll weigh about twenty pounds," he decided. "Yes; undoubtedly it's the fellow Thomas shot last night. The brute was so badly wounded that he was unable to drag himself far away."

"What shall we do with him now?" asked the boys.

"Take him to camp and leave him till Lige returns," advised the Professor." And I think we had better tie up our young friend Stacy, or he will be getting into more mischief than we are able to get him out of."

"Why can't we skin the cat?" inquired Ned.

"I should think you would prefer to wait till the guide sees it. And, besides, he knows better how to do that than any of the rest of us."

"Are - are bob-cats good to eat?" asked Chunky sheepishly.

The boys shouted.

"Not satisfied with trying to kill the poor beast, now you want to eat him," jeered Ned Rector. "Why, Stacy Brown, you ought to be ashamed of yourself. No, I never heard of any one with an appetite so difficult to satisfy that he was willing to eat cats -- "

"Yes; but this isn't a real cat," protested Stacy.

"You would have found him real enough if he had fastened one of those ugly claws in your flesh," laughed Tad.

"Eat him, by all means, then," advised Ned. "Eat him raw. I wouldn't even stop to cook the beast if I were in your place."

Walter and Stacy picked up the dead animal, carrying it along through the bushes, all talking loudly, the boys - though they would have been slow to admit the fact - casting envious glances at the fat boy and his trophy. Chunky told himself he would have something to write to the folks back East that would make them open their eyes.

The boys, after having reached the camp, stretched the cat out on a flat rock. And now that the animal lay in the full light of day, the sight of its ugly, beetling brow, thin, cruel lips and powerful teeth made each of the three boys feel rather thankful that he had not had the luck to come face to face with it over in the bushes.

As for Chunky, he sat down beside the cat to enjoy the proud sense of victory, gazing down at the trophy with fascinated eyes. Deep down in his heart, he wondered how he ever had had the courage to attack it. But, of course, Chunky confided nothing of this to his companions.

"Congratulating yourself, eh!" laughed Ned Rector.

Chunky glanced up at him solemnly.

"At this minute I was wishing I had a piece of apple pie," he answered, hitching his belt a little tighter.

# CHAPTER XII

## ROUGH RIDERS IN THE SADDLE

The afternoon had grown old when a distant "C-oo-ee-e," told them that Lige Thomas was on his way back to camp.

They answered his call with a wild whoop, and were for rushing off to meet him. But Professor Zepplin advised them to remain where they were and get the fire going in case Lige had failed to find the pack train. He no doubt would bring food of some kind with him. The fire would be ready and thus no time would be lost in preparing the first meal of the day, which, in this case, would be breakfast, dinner and supper all in one.

The boys awaited the guide's approach with impatience, some pacing back and forth, while others coaxed the fire into a roaring blaze, at the same time confiding to each other how hungry they were.

After what had seemed an interminable time they heard Jose urging along the lazy burros.

It was a gladsome sound to this band of hungry boys, whose ordinarily healthy appetites, under the bracing mountain air and the long fast, had taken on what the Professor described as a "razor edge."

"Now you may go," he nodded.

With a shout, the boys dashed pell-mell to meet the pack train, and, falling in behind the slow-moving burros, urged them on with derisive shouts and sundry resounding slaps on the animals' flanks.

"Had anything to eat!" asked the guide.

"Not enough to give us indigestion," answered Ned. "Cold water is the most nourishing thing we've touched since last night."

"But I left you a rabbit. Didn 't you find it?"

"We did not. It must have come to life some time during the night and dug its way out," laughed Tad.

"And we've got a surprise for you," announced Stacy, swelling with pride.

"What's it all about?" laughed the guide.

"You'll see when you get to camp," answered Chunky. "I don't need guns to hunt with. A stout club for mine."

After having shown the cat to Lige and getting his promise to teach them how to skin it, the boys set to with a will to assist in the unpacking. While they were pitching the tents over the pine cots Jose got out his Buzzacot range, which he started up in the open, and in a few moments the savory odors of the cooking reached the nostrils of the Pony Riders, drawing from them a shout of approval.

By the time the meal was ready the tents had been

pitched and the boys had returned from the spring, rubbing their faces with their coarse towels, their cheeks glowing and their eyes sparkling in anticipation of the feast.

Chunky reached the table first, greedily surveying what had been placed on it.

"Hooray, fellows!" he shouted. "Hot biscuit and - and honey. What do you think of that?"

"Honey? Why, Mr. Thomas, where did you get honey?" asked Walter.

"Found a bee tree on my way back, and cut it down. I think you will find there is enough of it to double you all up," grinned Lige.

"We'll take all chances," advised Ned. "But what's this! It looks like jam."

"Jam?" exclaimed Chunky, stretching his neck and eyeing the dish longingly.

"Yes; wild plum jam," answered the guide.

"Wow!" chuckled Stacy under his breath.

"Now, fall to, young gentlemen," directed the Professor. "I am free to admit that I am hungry, too. I think I shall help myself to some of that wild plum jam and biscuit, first It reminds me of old times. We sometimes had jam when I was with the German -- "

"Army," added Ned.

"Yes."

But the Professor was lost in his enjoyment of the biscuit, which he had liberally smeared with the delicious jam.

Chunky did even better than that. He buried his biscuit under a layer of jam, over which he spread a thick coating of honey.

Ned fixed him with a stern eye.

"Remember, sir, that a certain amount of dignity befits the office of president of the Pony Riders Club, "he said.

Chunky colored.

"It's good, anyway."

"Then, I think I'll try some myself," announced Ned, helping himself liberally to the honey and jam. "I'd lose my dignity for a mouthful of that, any day," he decided after having sampled the combination. "President Brown, I withdraw my criticism. I offer you my humble apologies. You are not only the champion hunter of the Pony Riders, but you also are the champion food selector and eater. Next thing we know you'll be providing us with bear steak."

"Bears, did you say?" demanded Stacy in a voice not unmixed with awe. "Are there bears up here?"

"I reckon there are," smiled the guide. "We are in the bear country now. I had a tough battle with one in a cave not far from here, several years ago. I came near losing my life too, and -- "

"A cave?" interrupted Tad.

"Yes, the country is full of caves. Some of them are so big that you would lose yourself in them almost at once; while others are merely dens where bears and other animals live. Besides this, there are many abandoned mines up the range further. All are more or less interesting, and some, for various reasons, are dangerous to enter."

"Shall we see any of them?" asked Tad eagerly.

"All you want. Perhaps we may even explore some if we come across any," said the guide.

This announcement filled the boys with excitement.

"What I want to know, is, when do we go hunting?" asked Ned.

"That depends. Perhaps Tuesday. We shall need a dog. But I know an old settler who will lend us his dog, if it is not out. Of course, dogs can't follow the trail of an animal as well, now, as they could with snow on the ground. But this dog, you will find, is a wonder. He can ride a pony, or do almost anything that you might set him at."

"I think I'll ride my own pony and let the dog walk," announced Ned.

Supper having been finished, the party gathered about the camp fire for their evening chat, after which, admonishing Stacy to keep within his tent and not to go borrowing trouble, the boys turned in for a sound sleep.

As yet, they had been unable to attempt any fancy riding with their ponies, owing to the rugged nature of the country through which they had been journeying. So in the morning they asked Lige if he knew of a place where they could do some "stunts," as Ned Rector phrased it.

The guide said that, by making a detour in their journey that day, they would cross table lands several acres in extent and covered with grass.

"And come to think of it, that will be an ideal place for us to drop off for our noon meal," he added. "We'll let Jose go on again, and I don't think he can lose himself so easily this time. The trail is so plainly marked that he can't miss it."

The boys were now all anxiety to start, while the ponies, after their Sunday rest, were almost as full of life as were their owners. The little animals were becoming more sure-footed every day, and Ned said that, before the trip was finished, "Jimmie" would be able to walk a slack rope.

An early start was made, so that the party reached the promised table lands shortly before ten o'clock in the forenoon. A temporary camp was quickly pitched.

At their urgent request, Professor Zepplin told the boys to go ahead and enjoy themselves.

"But be careful that you don't break your necks," he added, with a laugh. "I guess I had better go along to see that you do not."

They assured him that nothing was further from their intention, and quickly casting aside guns and cartridge belts, they threw themselves into their saddles again for a jolly romp.

The great, green field, surrounded on all sides by tall trees, made the place an ideal one for their purpose.

"Tell you what let's do," suggested Tad. "Suppose we start with a race? We'll race the length of the field and back. We'll do it three times, and the one who wins two times out of three will be it."

To this all agreed. Appointing Professor Zepplin as starter, the Pony Riders lined up for the word.

The first heat was run easily, none of the ponies being put to its utmost speed. Walter Perkins won the heat.

The next two heats were different. This time the battle lay between Tad Butler and Ned Rector. It was a beautiful race, the little Indian ponies seeming to enter thoroughly into the spirit of the contest, stretching themselves out to their full lengths, and, with heads on a level with their backs, fairly flew across the great plot of green.

Up to within a moment of the finish of the second heat the two ponies were racing neck and neck.

Tad hitched in his saddle a little, throwing the greater part of his weight on the stirrups. He slapped Texas sharply on the flank with the flat of his hand.

Texas seemed to leap clear of the ground, planting himself on all fours just over the line, the winner by a neck.

The third heat was merely a repetition of the second. All agreed that Tad's superior horsemanship, alone, had won the race for him. Ned took his defeat good-naturedly.

By this time, the boys had come to feel fully as much at home in the saddle as they formerly had been out of it. Even Stacy Brown, though he did not sit his saddle with the same grace that marked the riding of Tad Butler and Ned Rector, more practiced horsemen, was nevertheless no mean rider.

"We will now try some cowboy riding," announced Tad, who, as master of horse, was supposed to direct the riding of the club. "Who of you can pick up a hat on the run?"

"Don't all speak at once," said Ned, after a moment's silence on the part of the band.

"I'll show you," promised Tad.

Galloping into camp the boy fetched his sombrero, which he carried well out into the field and tossed away. Then, bidding the boys ride up near the spot to watch him, he drew off some ten rods, and, wheeling, spurred his pony to a run.

Tad rose in the stirrups as he neared the spot where the hat lay, keeping his eyes fixed intently upon it.

All at once he dropped to the saddle and slipped the

left foot from the stirrup. Grasping the pommel with the left hand, he appeared to dive head first toward the ground.

They saw his long hair almost brush the grass; one of his hands swept down and up, and once more Tad Butler rose standing, in his stirrups, uttering a cowboy yell as he waved the sombrero on high.

The boys howled with delight - that is, all did save Stacy Brown.

"Huh! That's nothing. I can do that myself," he grunted. "I've seen them do that in the wild west shows too many times not to know how myself."

Walter smiled, with a twinkle in his eyes.

"Why not show us, then?" he said.

"I will," replied Chunky, confidently.

"Got your life insured?" asked Ned. "If you haven't I would advise you to go easy. Tad is an experienced rider."

"Don't you worry about me, Ned Rector. Guess I know how to ride. Let me have that hat, Tad," he demanded as the latter came trotting up to the group.

Stacy, his face flushed, determination plainly showing in his eyes, stretched forth his hand for the sombrero. Riding bravely out into the field, he tossed it to the ground. The first time he rode swiftly by it, leaning over to look at the hat as he passed, holding to the pommel firmly with his left hand.

Stacy dismounted and removed the hat carefully to one side.

"What's that for?" demanded Ned, wonderingly.

"Hat too close to me. I couldn't get it," explained Chunky.

The boys roared.

"Why don't you move the pony? You don't have to move the hat, you ninny."

Once more Stacy approached the sombrero, his pony running well, and as he drew near it, they saw him rise in his saddle just as Tad Butler had done a few minutes before.

"By George, he's going to try it," exclaimed Ned.

"Be careful, Chunky," warned Walter.

"He's got to learn," declared Tad.

Then Chunky essayed the feat.

At the moment when he freed his left foot from the stirrup, he threw his body sharply to the right, reaching for the hat without taking the precaution to grasp the pommel.

As a result, instead of stopping when he reached the hat, the boy kept on going. Fortunately, his right foot freed itself from the stirrup at the same time, or there might have been a different ending. Chunky turned a double somersault, lay still for a moment, then struggled up, rubbing his body gingerly, as the rest of the party came hurrying up to him.

"Are you hurt?" asked Tad apprehensively.

"No; that's the way I always get off," grinned Chunky.

# CHAPTER XIII

## VISIONS OF GOLD

After satisfying themselves that Stacy was not injured, the others of the party each made an effort to pick up the hat, though with much more caution than Stacy had used.

Ned accomplished the trick the first time he tried. Walter, however, made several attempts, instructed by Tad, before he finally caught the knack of it.

"That will do for one day," decided the instructor, finally. "We must not tire out our ponies, for we still have a long jaunt ahead of us, according to the guide."

When they reached the camp, Stacy was still rubbing his head, much to the amusement of his companions. The noonday lunch was a light one; while they were eating it the ponies were tethered out on the plain to browse on the fresh, green grass.

Shortly after noon the party was on its way again, Lige being anxious to reach their destination before dark. Yet the trail was so rugged and precipitous that rapid progress was impossible. To add to this, late in the afternoon they overtook the pack train, which they found halted in the trail. One of the burros had gone lame, nor did Jose know what the trouble was. He was sitting by the side of the trail helplessly, waiting for someone to come along.

Tad hastily slipped from his saddle, running over to the burro.

"Which foot is he lame in?" asked the boy.

"Donno," answered the Mexican.

The boy led the little animal back and forth several times.

"It's the off hind foot," he announced.

"Off?" queried Chunky. "He doesn't seem to have a foot off."

"No, I didn't mean that. Horsemen call the right the off side, and the left the near one," explained Tad, picking up the beast's foot and examining it critically.

"He has stepped on a sharp piece of rock and driven it into the hoof," announced the boy. "I am afraid we shall have to unload the pack and strap him down before I can get it out."

Tying their horses, all hands drew near to witness the proceeding, which bade fair to be unusually interesting. However, Tad skilfully rigged a harness out of a long piece of quarter-inch rope. This he put on the burro, and soon had the animal on its knees, then on its side. The rope was drawn taut so that the burro could not kick, after which the boy cautiously cut around the sharp stone with his pocket knife, and, after considerable effort, extracted it.

"I'm sorry we have nothing to put in the wound. But I guess he will go along all right. He'll be lame for the rest of the day; but we cannot help that."

Once more they loaded up the beast of burden and the procession continued on its way, Lige having decided to keep the train in sight in case it was thought advisable to stop and make camp. They had been so delayed that it was now close to sunset.

At dusk they were still some distance from their destination.

"I think we bad better pull up here," suggested the guide.

"There's a moon up there," answered Tad. "Why not go on by moonlight? That is, of course, if you can follow the trail."

"I could follow the trail with my eyes shut, young man," grinned the guide. "What do you say, Professor?"

"As you think best, Lige. I do not mind a moonlight ride."

"Yes; let's go on," urged the boys, looking forward with keen anticipation to traveling over the mountains by night, for this they had not yet had an opportunity to do.

"Very well, if your appetites will keep for another hour or so. We should make it in an hour and a half," Lige decided, glancing about him keenly for landmarks. "We'll try, at any rate."

The shadows now began to close in, the gulches standing out in bold relief, black, forbidding seas at the foot of the ridges that lay a white wonderland in the moonlight.

"This is great!" declared Ned enthusiastically.

"Glorious," breathed Tad, drinking in the scene with wide open eyes, while inhaling in long, slow breaths, the soft mountain air. "I never saw anything more beautiful."

Now that night had settled over the trail, the riders had to move along more cautiously, and with tight reins, that their ponies might not stumble and hurl the riders over their heads. Tad, with an eye to caution, had advised them to do this. In this way the train moved on until nearly nine o'clock, when Lige announced that they had reached their halting place.

The mountain top where they stopped was thickly studded with cedars and pinyon trees, while off in the ravines slender spruces reared their sharp points above the shadows, projecting up through the black sea like the spars of a whole fleet of sunken schooners.

"Old Ben Tackers lives nigh here," the guide told them. "I'll go over and get him after supper. We can then talk with him about his dog. He can tell us all about the game. Ben is a character. However, you mustn't mind his blunt way of speaking. The old fellow is all right at heart."

Ben came over later in the evening, and the boys were much interested in him. A thick shock of shaggy hair covered his head and face, while through the mass of gray and brown twinkled a pair of bright, beady eyes. Ned said they reminded him of a couple of burnt holes in a horse blanket,

"Any game about here, Mr. Tackers?" asked Ned after the old mountaineer had been introduced to them.

"For them as can see, there's things to be seen," answered Ben enigmatically. "What do you reckon on shooting?"

"Anything we can find to shoot at," answered Ned.

"Beckon I'll go home and lock up my pigs, then," declared the old man firmly.

"Oh, it's not as bad as that, sir," hastily added Tad. "My friend, Ned, means anything in the game line. Surely we can be trusted to tell the difference between a bob-cat and a litter of pigs. Stacy Brown, here, knocked out a bobcat with nothing but a club at Beaver Mountain yesterday."

Ben turned to look at Chunky, who, huddled on the ground, appeared not unlike a large, round ball.

"Huh! He ain't much to look at," grunted the old man. "I got a tame cub over to my cabin that would be a good mate for him."

Stacy flushed painfully.

"Mr. Thomas was saying that you might be willing to

make some arrangement with us so we could use your dog for a few days," hinted Professor Zepplin.

"Eh! Dogs! Lige Thomas kin have my dogs - I've got two of them now. No arrangement ain't necessary," growled Ben.

"We prefer to pay for them, sir," spoke up Walter. "And perhaps you may be able to tell us, also, where we may hope to find game?"

"Mebby so and mebby not. I'll see Lige about that. Got that cat skin ye was talking about?" he demanded suddenly, looking from one to the other.

Chunky brought it out, the old man examining it critically, nodding his head over some thought of his own.

"Bigger cats on Tacker's mountain," he grunted. "Want to sell it?" Chunky shook his head.

"Huh!" exclaimed the old man, rising and starting away.

"What's your hurry, sir?" asked the Professor politely.

"Must shut up the pigs. The little red-faced bear over there by the fire might get loose with his club again," and the mountaineer strode from the camp without another word.

Stacy Brown hung his head in chagrin, while the boys laughed heartily at what they considered a most excellent joke on Stacy.

"Chatty old person, isn't he, Mr. Thomas?" grinned Ned.

"Well, not exactly. But he's one of the best hunters on the Park Range. Besides, he is credited with knowing more about what's hidden under these mountains than any other man on them. But Ben doesn't care much for money. He'll set us right about the game when the time comes. If the game is not running he'll stay away and say nothing. However, at the right moment, you'll see old Ben Tackers and his dogs suddenly appearing in camp. It will do you no good to ask him questions. He'll tell me in a word what he has to say, and I shall have to guess the rest."

"And you will know what he means?" asked Tad.

"I reckon," grinned Lige.

"In about the same way he told me to-night that there were some bad men in these parts - prospectors they called themselves - who were trying to locate some sort of a claim -- "

"Claim? What kind?" asked Walter.

"Gold."

"Gold? Here?" spoke up the Professor sharply.

"Mountains are full of it, if you can find it," answered Lige in an impressive tone.

And the boys, thrilled by the thought that perhaps fortunes in the bright yellow metal lay beneath their feet, went to bed to dream of buried treasures and limitless wealth.

# CHAPTER XIV

## A NARROW ESCAPE

The Pony Riders awoke full of enthusiasm for the work of the day. Thus far, each day had held a new and wonderful experience for them, while those to come were destined to be even more full of stirring incidents.

Most of all, the boys looked forward to the hunting trips that had been promised. Next to that came the exploration of mountain caves. It was enough to gladden the heart of any boy.

Immediately they had arisen, they descended upon the guide in a body, demanding to know if they were to hunt that day.

"Depends upon Ben Tackers," answered Lige. "You remember what I told you last night. He'll let us know when it's time for our little excursion. I think we had best have another hour of target practice this morning."

This plan suited the boys so exactly that, after breakfast, they set to work cleaning their rifles. A dozen rounds of ammunition were placed in their cartridge belts, after which, the boys announced their readiness for practice.

"Get the ponies," directed the guide.

"Ponies? What for? We're not going to shoot the ponies, are we?" asked Ned Rector.

"I wouldn't advise it," grinned the guide. "I'll show you what I want after we have reached the range. I suppose you know that hunting in this country is quite generally done on horseback, so you will have to get used to that way of shooting. Also your ponies must become accustomed to the firing from their backs. Snap shooting on horseback is a trick you will have to learn. It may be the means of saving your lives some time when you are after wild game."

The boys made a rush to the spot where the ponies were staked. The little animals looked up in mild protest as their owners hastily threw on saddles, cinched the girths and slipped the bits into unwilling mouths.

Leading their ponies into camp, each boy, with gun slung over his shoulder, stood at the left of his mount, awaiting the command of his leader.

"Ready," announced Tad.

Four right hands grasped the saddle pommels, the left hands the manes.

"Mount!"

Four enthusiastic lads swung lightly into their saddles, gathering up the reins, and on the alert for the next command.

"Forward!" ordered Tad.

The Pony Riders clucked to the little animals and in single column filed slowly up the mountain pass.

The place that Lige Thomas had chosen for the target work was not an ideal one, being rough and uneven. Yet, as he explained to them, it represented general hunting conditions in the Rockies.

However, the boys did not care. Their ponies were sure-footed enough now, they thought, to warrant being trusted under ordinary conditions, while the boys themselves had no fear of their own ability to stick to their saddles.

Lige picked out a stump for the first target, on which he pinned a torn piece of newspaper.

This the boys were to shoot at with their ponies at the gallop. They were first to ride to the upper end of the range, after which, they were to gallop down the field, keeping to the right of the target, firing at will at any time before reaching a certain point designated by a handkerchief tied to a bush.

It was a proud and happy band that thundered down the field on the fleet-footed ponies, one at a time, discharging their weapons as they came bravely on.

At first the little animals objected, in no uncertain manner, to the crashing of the heavy guns over their heads. Chunky's horse reared and plunged until the boy was forced to drop his rifle and hang on desperately, while the pony tore about the field. The young man undoubtedly would have come to grief had not Tad

Butler, observing that his companion had lost control of the animal, put spurs to Texas, and reining alongside of Stacy, grasped the pony by the bit, subduing it only after a lively struggle. During this contest Chunky had let go of the reins entirely, and was clinging to the pommel of the saddle with both hands.

"You take Texas and let me ride your pony for a couple of rounds," suggested Tad. "I'll see if I can't trim him into shape."

Stacy willingly relinquished his horse, and Tad, mounting the stubborn little animal, treated the party to as entertaining a bit of horsemanship as they ever had witnessed. After Tad had finished with the pony the animal, thoroughly subdued, made no further objections to the discharge of weapons all about and over him.

"Now, go ahead, Chunky," advised Tad. "If he cuts up any more just take a tight rein and give him the spur. But I think he'll be good without it."

Stacy had no further trouble with the pony after that. In fact, all the ponies soon accustomed themselves to the noise of the firing and the attendant excitement.

At first none of the boys seemed able to hit even the stump. Presently, though, little black patches began to appear on the white paper as the marksmen dashed by, each successful shot being greeted by a cheer of approval from the spectators.

"Those boys have the right stuff in them," said the guide to Professor Zepplin. "They shoot and ride like old hands already, though they don't hit the mark every time they shoot"

They are young Americans," smiled the Professor. "No other country in the world produces such types. As a foreigner I can appreciate that."

While they were talking, Tad was taking his turn at the target.

"Just look at that boy ride. That proves it," said the Professor.

Tad had dropped the bridle rein over the saddle bow as he neared the shooting mark. Rising in his stirrups, riding there as if he were a part of the animal itself, he was holding the bobbing rifle easily, eyes fixed on the mark that hung gleaming in the sunlight.

Suddenly the butt of the rifle sprang to his right shoulder, a flash of smoke and flame leaped from the muzzle of the gun, and a tiny black patch appeared, like magic, fairly in the center of the target.

Dropping to his saddle, half-turning his body, Tad Butler sent back a second shot hard on the report of the first one, once more planting a leaden pellet in the now well-riddled paper.

The boys sent up a whoop of approval.

"I guess that will do for to-day," decided the guide. "Got any charges left in your magazines?"

"I have," answered Chunky.

"Draw them, then."

"Yes," said Ned Rector. "Even though Chunky is beginning to get his eyes open, I don't consider myself safe so long as he has a loaded gun in his hands. What we shall do with him when we get after real game, and can't watch him every second, I don't know."

"Don't you bother about me. You've got enough to do looking after yourself," retorted Stacy sharply, much to the discomfiture of his tormentor.

The boys now turned campward, well satisfied with the morning's practice and with keen appetites for the noonday meal. Nothing had been seen of Ben Tackers, so their hopes for going hunting that day were shattered.

Yet they were given no opportunity to brood over their disappointment. Professor Zepplin and Lige Thomas still had a few surprises in store for them. Very cleverly, they had pieced these surprises along instead of giving them all to the lads at the beginning. Thus each day held its new interest, different from any that had preceded it.

"We will call this our shooting day, eh, Thomas?" smiled the Professor significantly.

"It has been."

"Then, perhaps you had best get out the other implements of warfare for our young gentlemen. It will keep them busy until supper time, furnishing something new as well."

With a knowing grin, Lige went to the cook tent, soon returning with an armful. At first the boys glanced at the bundle curiously, then with more interest as it began to assume shape and form to their eyes.

"What -- what -- " stammered Tad.

Stacy, whose eyes were wide open, was the first to recognize the articles, and as he did so, Lige dumped them on the ground.

"Bows and arrows," cried the boys, performing a grotesque war dance about the weapons.

"We'll be real Indians now, won't we?" chortled Chunky.

"They are only playthings," sniffed Ned. "What good are they when we have real rifles?"

"You'll find these bows and arrows real enough," answered the guide. "They were made by Indians, and some of them have been used by Indians, not only for hunting, but against men as well. A shot from one of those arrows might put an end to any one of you fully as quickly as would a bullet from one of your thirty-eights."

"Shall we help ourselves?" asked Ned.

"Wait. I'll divide them according to your size and strength. These two are war bows. I think I'll give them to Master Tad and Ned Rector. It takes a strong arm to pull them, and you'll want to be careful which way you shoot."

"I'll show you fellows how to shoot," averred

Stacy. "I can beat any boy in the bunch with the bow and arrow. I learned the trick up in New England, where I come from. My ancestors learned it from the Indians, who used to shoot them up, and the trick has been handed down in my family. Somebody throw up his hat and see me pink it," he directed, stringing his bow skilfully.

The boys could not repress a smile at Chunky's self-praise.

"Here you go," said Ned, sending his sombrero spinning high in the air, hoping thereby to take Stacy so much by surprise that he would be unable to draw a bead on it.

But Chunky demonstrated that, however slow he might be in some other things, he could twang a bow with remarkable skill.

Even before the hat had spent its upward flight, Stacy Brown's bowstring sang, a slender dark streak sped through the air, its course laid directly for the hat of which its owner was so proud.

"Hi there! Look out! You're going to hit it!" warned Ned.

That was exactly what Stacy had intended to do, though none had had the slightest idea that he could shoot well enough to accomplish the feat.

To their astonishment, the keen-pointed arrow went fairly into the center of the hat, coming out at the crown, its feathered butt tearing a great rent in the peak of the sombrero as it passed through.

Ned groaned as he witnessed the disaster that had come upon his new hat. But he got no sympathy from the rest of the boys.

"I'll trade with you. You can wear mine," consoled Chunky, observing his companion's rueful countenance as he picked up the sombrero, sorrowfully surveying the rent in its peak. "I'll do nothing of the sort," snapped Ned. "I told you to shoot at it. It serves me right and I'll take my medicine like a man. If it rains, I'll stuff the hole full of leaves," he added humorously. "Then my umbrella will be just as good as yours."

"That's the talk," approved the boys. "Anybody else want to offer his hat to the sacrifice!" grinned Chunky.

"I think hereafter you had better use the blunt arrows unless you are shooting at game," advised the guide. "Those flint arrow heads are dangerous things for work such as yours. I'll pack them away, so there will be no danger of an accident."

After having practiced in camp for a time, the boys strayed off, hoping for a chance to try their skill on some live thing. To this the Professor made no objection, for they were now becoming so used to the mountains as to be quite well able to take care of themselves, unless they got too far from camp, which they were not likely to do.

Tad soon strolled away by himself, taking a course due south by his pocket compass. This led him directly over the range where they had been shooting earlier in the day, and the boy smiled with pride as he passed the target and counted up the bullet holes that his own rifle had made. He then pressed on, intending to enter the cedar forest that crowned a great ridge some distance beyoud him.

Before reaching there, however, Tad sat down in a rocky basin, to enjoy to the fullest the sense of being alone in the mountain fastness. His quiver was full of arrows, and the strong, business-like looking bow lay across his knees.

"If I could see a bob-cat now, I'd have something real to interest me," Tad confided to himself.

But not a sign of animal life did he observe anywhere about him.

Tad's right hand was resting on a small jagged stone beside him. It felt cool under his touch, and, after a little, the boy carelessly picked it up and looked at it. As he gazed, his eyes took on a different expression. The stone, in spots, sparkled brilliantly in the sunlight. He turned it over and over, examining it critically.

"I wonder if it is gold?" marveled the boy, his eyes growing large with wonder. "I'll take it back to camp and ask Lige."

Tad scrambled to his feet, but ere he could carry out his purpose of starting for camp, an unexpected and startling thing happened.

There was a whir, as of some object being hurled through the air. The boy experienced a stinging sensation on his right cheek, as the missile grazed it, and a stone the size of a man's hand clattered to the rocks several feet ahead of him, rolling over and over, finally toppling from a small cliff.

Some one had thrown the stone at him. Had it hit the boy's head fairly it almost surely would have killed him. Tad Butler needed no other evidence than that afforded by his own senses to tell him the missile was intended for him.

He whirled sharply. But not a person was in sight. All at once, however, the keen-eyed boy discovered a slight movement in the sage brush, a few rods to the rear of where he had been sitting.

Like a flash he whipped a blunt arrow from the quiver.

The bow twanged viciously, and the arrow sped straight into the sage brush. A yell of rage and a floundering about in the bush as if someone were running, told the boy that his shot had reached a human mark.

Pacing the sage, Tad had become conscious of the fact that before him lay a large black hole in the rocks, and he dimly realized that he had come upon a cave. But he gave the matter no further attention at that moment, his first thought being that he must get back to camp as quickly as possible.

Stringing his bow, Tad hurled another arrow into the brush, then bounded away, wondering vaguely who his mysterious enemy might be.

# CHAPTER XV

## THE BATTLE IN THE CAVE

Reaching the rifle range, Tad sat down to think over the occurrences of the past half hour. Why anyoue should wish to do him harm, he could not understand. And, if anyoue did, why should he adopt such a peculiar way of attack? Had it been a mountaineer, Tad was sure the man would have used a gun instead of standing off and throwing stones at turn like a petulant school boy. He realized too, that they had a different mode of procedure in the mountains.

"I'd have been as dead as Chunky's bob-cat if the stone had hit me fairly," muttered the boy. "Anyway, I've got a chunk of something that looks a good deal like gold, in my pocket," he added.

Deciding to say nothing about his recent experience to his companions, Tad strolled slowly toward camp. Yet, he had firmly made up his mind to go back to the spot later and make sure that his suspicions were correct.

Most of the boys had returned by the time Tad arrived, and there was a clamor to know the result of his hunting trip.

"Maybe I shot a cat. But, I didn't," he grinned.

"What's that!" demanded Ned.

"Anyway, I've brought back a chunk of gold and discovered a cave. That's more than the rest of you have done, I'll warrant."

Either announcement would have been sufficient to arouse the interest of the campers, and they crowded about Tad, demanding to know what he meant by his mysterious words.

"I found a cave, I tell you," he repeated.

"Where?" asked Lige.

Tad explained its location as well as he could.

"And I found this chunk of gold, too," he added proudly.

The guide took the piece of ore, examining it carefully.

"That isn't gold," he laughed. "That is what is known as 'fools' gold.'"

"Scientifically known as 'iron pyrites'" explained the Professor.

Tad's jaw fell at this shattering of his hopes. Yet, when Lige tossed the piece of mineral on the ground, the boy picked it up and dropped it back in his pocket. Why he did this he did not know. Perhaps it was instinct. However, after a few moments he had forgotten all about it.

"You must have had a fight with a bob-cat to get that

fierce scratch on your cheek," chuckled Ned Rector. "I must say that Chunky has you beaten to a - a - I've forgotten the word I want - when it conies to fighting cats."

"I have seen no cats to-day, Ned. But I have found a real cave. Will you take us over to explore it, in the morning, Mr. Thomas? I'll show you the biggest thing of its kind you ever have seen, if you'll go," promised Tad, enthusiastically.

"Providing we don't go hunting, yes, and - and find some more fools' gold," laughed the guide.

Tad went to his tent, for the wound in his cheek was giving him considerable pain, and a glance into the hand mirror showed him that the cheek was beginning to swell.

Taking a towel with him, the boy hurried off to a mountain rivulet, where he bathed the wounded cheek, holding the wet towel to it to reduce the swelling.

Chancing to look up, he observed the guide, Lige Thomas, standing before him, eyeing him keenly.

"Warm, isn't?" grinned Tad.

"Rather. Put the towel down. I want to look at that cheek."

Tad hesitated, drew the towel away, and gazed back at the guide with a challenge in his eyes.

Lige examined the wound carefully.

"How'd you get it?" he demanded, straightening up.

"Why do you ask that? It's only a scratch."

"Because I want to know. If you do not wish to tell me, of course I shall not press you. However, it will be my duty to call the attention of the Professor to it. You see, I am responsible for you boys while you are up here, and -- "

"A stone did it," interrupted Tad, with a touch of stubbornness in his tone.

"A stone?"

"Yes."

"How?"

"Somebody threw it at me."

For a moment the guide gazed at Tad doubtingly.

"I'll tell you all about it," exclaimed Tad impetuously. "But promise me that you won't tell the boys. They'd never cease joking me about it. I'm going back there to-morrow to see if I can find the fellow who shied the rock at me. No; I didn't see him at all. I was sitting with my back to him when he let fly at me. But I pinked him, Mr. Thomas. Believe me, I did -- "

"Pinked him?"

"Yes, I let him have an arrow full tilt, and I know it hit him, for he yelled and ran away," explained the boy.

"This matter must be looked into," decided Lige thoughtfully. "It begins to look as if Ben Tackers was right about the gang after all. No; I'll not say anything to the crowd. It would only stir them up. We will visit the cave to-morrow, and, while the others are amusing themselves, you and I will look the ground over a bit. I'll go back now, and you may come along when you get ready."

Tad remained by the stream until he heard the supper call, whereupon he rose slowly and picked his way over the rocks to where the others had assembled about the table in the gathering twilight.

The boy's appetite, however, had not been affected by the experience through which he had passed that afternoon, and he stowed away a hearty meal, after which the evening was spent in listening to stories of the chase related by Lige Thomas.

There being still no sign of Ben Tackers on the following morning, a visit to the cave was decided upon. They reached the place about nine o'clock, guided by Tad, who took them to the hole in the rock at once.

"I guess you boys had better fix up some torches," directed Lige. "Sometimes there are holes within holes, in these mountains, and we don't want to take a sudden drop down a hundred feet or so. Three torches will be enough to light. You had better take along two or three more in case of need."

Before entering, the guide took the precaution of unslinging his rifle, and, placing the boys behind him with the torches, he entered the cave first. They were obliged to stoop to get through the opening. Once within they followed what appeared to be a passage hewn out of the solid rock.

"Ah, here we are!" exclaimed Lige finally, straightening and glancing about him curiously.

They found themselves in a dome-like chamber, from which hung suspended hundreds of stalactites that threw back the rays of the torches in a thousand sparkling, scintillating points of fire.

The Pony Riders gasped in amazement. Never had any of them seen anything like this.

"Wha - what is it?" breathed Tad Butler.

"Stalactites," announced the Professor.

"Look like icicles to me. B-r-r-r," shivered Stacy Brown.

"It is a very common thing to find them in caves," added the Professor. "But I never have had the pleasure of observing the formation before."

"I can show you some better than these," stated the guide. "I know of a cave, not so very far from here, that is as big as a church, and a regular picture of one, too."

"Is this the end of the cave?" asked Ned.

"No; there are other passages leading further into the mountain, at the other end of the chamber there," replied Lige.

"Are we going to explore them?" inquired Walter.

"Yes; we can go further, if you wish. But you boys must keep a sharp lookout where you are going. Don't fool too much. It's easy to get into trouble here, you know."

While Lige was speaking, Tad had edged cautiously to one side of the chamber, where he had observed what appeared to be a small rock, glistening in the light of the torches. He picked it up, unobserved by the others, and dropped it into his pocket for further observation.

The party then pushed on into the cave, one chamber leading into another, forming a bewildering maze, the brilliant reflections almost blinding them at times, until at last Lige Thomas was forced to admit that he never had quite seen the like of it anywhere else in the Rockies.

"Didn't I tell you I'd show you the biggest thing you ever saw in your life?" glowed Tad Butler.

At that instant a yell of terror from Stacy Brown drew their attention sharply from Tad, their eyes bulging with fear at what they saw before them.

There, sitting on its haunches, paws extended menacingly, showing its teeth as it uttered low, angry growls of protest, was a full-grown black bear.

Tad Butler, indeed, had shown some of them the most surprising things they had ever seen. Yet this was not exactly the surprise he had planned for them, or for himself.

The guide had put his gun down as he entered the chamber, to get one of the stalactites for Professor Zepplin, who wished to examine it. As a result, Lige was now some twenty-five feet away from his weapon.

At first, with the bright reflection in his eyes, the guide was unable to understand what it was that had caused their sudden fright. Yet the breathless silence about him told him instantly that something serious had happened.

The bear had dropped to all fours and was lumbering straight toward Stacy Brown, who stood fascinated, watching the approach of the hideous object, whose raised upper lip showed a row of white gleaming teeth.

"Look out!" yelled Tad suddenly finding his voice.

"Quick, guide!" begged the Professor, weakly.

"What is it? Where?" snapped Lige, crouching down and shading his eyes to protect them from the glare.

He quickly saw what had caused the startling alarm. He saw too, the hulking beast drawing nearer and nearer to Stacy Brown, and knew that only some sudden shock to his mind would break the spell that seemed to possess the boy at that moment.

"Run!" thundered the guide.

But Chunky stood as rigid as a statue.

Lige sprang for his rifle. In his haste he slipped on the smooth, damp floor and went sprawling.

By the time he had recovered himself, the bear had ambled up to Stacy, until the boy could feel the hot, nauseating breath beating against his face.

Tad Butler without regard for his own safety, leaped for the bear. But Professor Zepplin was too quick for him. He caught Tad by the arm, jerking him back.

Now, at that instant, Stacy Brown did a thing that brought a groan from each one who witnessed the daring act.

Chunky drew back his pudgy fist and let go with all his might.

His knuckles smote the bear fairly on the point of its nose, and the impact sounded loud and clear in the tense stillness of the cave.

If the Pony Riders were surprised, Bruin was even more so. With a grunt the bear suddenly sat down on its haunches, passing its paws over its nose, bewilderment plainly written on its countenance. Under ordinary circumstances the boys would have laughed. But now they were too horrified to do so.

Chunky, either because he was emboldened by the success of his attack, or through the excitement of the moment, picked up a rock from the cave floor, and stepping back, hurled it with all his strength. The stone hit the bear a glancing blow on the head, bringing from the animal a growl of rage. Now, the brute was dangerously angered.

It charged the party savagely, jaws wide apart, but uttering no sound, not even a growl. By this time some one had pulled Chunky from his perilous position and Tad and Professor Zepplin were pushing the other boys back toward the exit with all possible haste. It all had happened in a few seconds. Lige scrambled to his feet, rifle in hand, just in time to see the big brute charging straight at him, as if recognizing that in that quarter lay its gravest danger.

There came a sudden flash of flame, a crash and a roar as if the very mountain had been rent in twain, followed by another and still another.

Tad had grabbed a torch from the hands of one of his companions, the instant Lige began to fire, and sprung back to give the guide sufficient light to shoot by.

In doing so, however, the boy had unwittingly placed himself in the direst peril.

The wounded bear was charging madly here and there, uttering terrific growls of mingled rage and pain. But the instant its bloodshot eyes were fixed upon the boy with the torch, the animal rose on its haunches, and, with paws making powerful sweeps in the air, bore down upon Tad.

The boy was too far over in the chamber to be able to make his escape without getting between Lige and the bear, and escape seemed well-nigh impossible

However, Tad did not lose his presence of mind. With a leap as unexpected as it was surprising, he sprang straight for the savage beast. It seemed as if he was throwing himself right into the wide open jaws to be crushed to death.

"Don't shoot!" he warned, leaping forward. As he did so, he lowered the torch to the level of his own eyes, and drove it straight into the gaping mouth of the maddened bear. Then Tad sprang lightly to one side, throwing himself prone upon the floor.

The great bear was not growling now, but its groans of agony as it fought to get the deadly thing from its throat, sent a chill to the hearts of all who heard them.

At the instant when Tad threw himself down, Lige pulled the trigger.

His bullet ploughed its way through the brain of the bear, relieving its fearful sufferings. Bruin collapsed and rolled over, dead.

# CHAPTER XVI

## LIVE CUBS CAPTURED

Bring torches!" shouted Lige. "Look out for yourselves! There may be another in the cave. This is an old she bear."

After the lights had been brought, the boys cautiously approached the dead bear. Lige was down on his knees examining it.

"I think we shall find something interesting here, before we have finished," he announced. "Master Tad, as you have strong nerves, you come along with me. The others can drag the bear out and wait for us outside. Bring a couple of extra torches, in case we need them."

"What are you looking for? More bear?" inquired the boy after they had penetrated further into the cave.

"You'll see; that is, if I find what I am looking for. Your cave is turning out better than any of us had any idea it would. Was that some more fools' gold you picked up back there?"

"Oh, you saw me, did you? I don't know. It shines, and that's all I know about it. Do you know of any place where there is real gold in this part of the Rockies?"

"Yes; there are some claims paying fairly well within twenty miles of here. The Lost Claim is supposed to be somewhere in this neighborhood, but thus far no one ever has been able to locate it. I've had suspicions that Ben Tackers might make a close guess if he wanted to disclose it. But old Ben wouldn't bother with the gold if it was dumped right down in his pig sty."

"What's the Lost Claim?"

"It's quite a long story. I'll tell it to you, briefly, while we are exploring the cave."

"Then it was a real gold mine?"

"It surely was, Master Tad. And I guess it is still. Some twenty years ago a miner who had been born and brought up in the Park Range began dropping down to Denver at more or less irregular intervals, where he exchanged nuggets of pure gold and pay dust for cash. The quality of the gold showed that it must come from a rich vein.

"Naturally, people were curious. But to all their questions, Ab Ferguson simply said he'd got the gold out of 'the Lost Claim.'"

"Wonder they didn't follow him. I should think they might have located it in that way?" wondered Tad.

"They did. But they might as well have tried to find the pot of gold that is said to be at one end or the other of the rainbow. Ab was too much of an Indian to be caught that way."

"What happened to him finally?"

"Knocked down by a runaway team in Denver, and died three days later."

"And he didn't tell anyoue where the Claim was?"

"Not he. They've been looking for it ever since. But no one, so far as I ever heard, has got anywhere near it. There's a bunch of hard characters beating up the mountains now, hoping to get rich without work. It's dollars to sandwiches they're hoping to find the Lost Claim."

"You - you don't suppose it was one of them who threw the stone at me, do you?" asked Tad reflectively.

"I hadn't thought of that. It may be - it may be. H-m-m-m. That's an idea."

"But why should they wish to harm me? I don't understand it at all."

"No more do I, unless they found you snooping about, or thought our party might be on the same lay they are. You know, fellows of that kind will stop at nothing. More than one man has been killed on nothing more than an idle suspicion, in these mountains. A lot more will follow in the same way. But we've been warned, and it will be well to keep a sharp lookout."

"If they hadn't thought we were near the Lost Claim, I don't see why they should have had any suspicions," decided Tad.

"On general principles - that's all."

"Did you ever try to find the Lost Claim?"

"I? Never. What would I do with it, if I had it? I'm like Ben Tackers - don't need any more money than I've got. More would be too much."

Yet Tad Butler was unable to rid his mind of the idea that somehow he had stumbled close upon the dead miner's secret. He determined to turn prospector at the very first opportunity.

"Is this more fools' gold?" he asked, pointing to a thin, yellow streak that sparkled in the rock at their right.

"I reckon it is. It has fooled more than one prospector, and drove some of them crazy. Take my advice and don't get the fever. Nothing but trouble will follow you if you do. Trouble always does follow the greed for the yellow metal."

They had been winding out in the maze of passages, Lige, in the meantime, keeping a sharp lookout for guide marks, now and then gouging a niche in the wall to guide them on their return journey.

"Watch out," he cautioned. "We are coming to something."

Sundry soft, muffled growls led them to proceed more carefully, until, finally, Lige directed the lad to raise the torch higher. Lige cocked his rifle, holding it in readiness for quick action. In this manner they crept further into the cave until Tad was suddenly startled by a loud laugh from the guide.

"What is it?" exclaimed the boy.

"Just what I thought. Come here."

At first, Tad could make nothing of what the guide was exhibiting.

However, after a moment's peering in that direction, the boy observed what appeared to be a round ball of fur in one corner of the chamber. "Wha - what is it - bears?" Lige nodded, and, striding over to the heap, he pulled it roughly apart. His act was greeted with a series of savage snarls and growls.

"Cubs. Four of them, and beauties, at that. I knew they were in here, somewhere, after I had examined the mother," announced the guide triumphantly.

"Bear cubs? You don't mean it!" exclaimed Tad joyously. "And we can take them with us?"

"That's exactly what we shall do. There will be one for each of you, and we can crate them up so they can be carried on the burros."

"One for each of us? Won't the boys go wild when they see them? But, how are we going to get them to camp?"

"I'll show you."

Taking a strip of rawhide from his pocket, Lige fashioned a collar about the neck of each cub, leaving a leash four or five feet long to lead the animal by. However, this was not accomplished without vigorous protest on the part of the cubs. Tad was highly amused at their efforts to cuff their captor with their little paws, which they wielded with more or less skill. Yet, they were too young to be able to make any great resistance, and the guide did not give the slightest attention to their attempts to drive them away.

"There," he announced, having secured the little animals. "We each will lead two. Don't be afraid to pull, if they hold back. They'll come along all right when they begin to choke."

With their prizes in tow Tad and the guide retraced their steps to the cave entrance.

At first, looks of amazement greeted them as they emerged with their strange captives.

"Know what they are?" grinned Tad, proudly hauling his cubs up for inspection.

The boys shook their heads.

"Bear cubs. There's one for each of us."

"Whoop!" shouted the boys in chorus.

"Now, we'll have a regular menagerie," exclaimed Ned. "If we could catch a live bob-cat to go with them, wouldn't that be great?"

"Will they bite?" asked Chunky, apprehensively edging away from one of the animals that was playfully tugging at his leggin.

"Not yet," answered the guide. "And you can tame them so they won't hurt you at all. They make good pets if one begins when they are young."

The next half hour was spent in skinning the big mother bear, which proceeding the boys watched with keen interest. Some of the meat they took back to camp with them to cook for supper.

They found old Ben Tackers there awaiting them.

"Hullo, Ben," greeted the guide. "How's everything?"

"Tol'ble," grunted the old mountaineer.

"Are the dogs ready?"

Ben nodded.

"Start morning," he said.

"Good," shouted the boys.

"We couldn't imagine where you had been keeping yourself all the time," added the Professor. "Lige went over to your cabin last night and found it locked."

"Been away, Ben?" asked Lige.

"Over to Eagle Pass. Miners steal old Ben's hogs - one, two of them. Sheriff come by-and-bye and chase bunch out. Old Ben kill them, but Sheriff do better. Big fight when Sheriff comes."

The boys laughed at his quaint way of expressing himself, but not catching the full import of his words.

Lige, on the other hand, eyed him questioningly; and, when Ben finally left the camp in his usual abrupt fashion, the guide rose and followed him. When Lige

Thomas returned, his face wore an expression of seriousness that amounted almost to anxiety.

The boys were excitedly discussing their plans for the morrow. It had been decided that the Professor should remain in camp with Jose, as, owing to the presence of the miners in the vicinity, it was not thought wise to leave the camp entirely alone. The four boys, with Lige Thomas, were to make the trip, from which, in case they found the game running, they might not return in twenty-four hours.

Tad had been thinking deeply. After a little while be rose and walked over to Professor Zepplin's tent.

"May I come in?" he asked.

"Certainly, walk right in, Tad. What is on your mind?"

"This," answered the lad, laying on the Professor's table the chunks of mineral that he had picked up.

"What's this? Ah, I see. More of the iron pyrites. The metal has driven many a poor fellow mad with anticipations of fabulous wealth," smiled the German.

"Are you sure it is fools' gold, Professor?"

"Reasonably so. But you may leave it here, if you wish, and I will examine it at my leisure. Where did you find the second piece?"

"In the cave. There is a streak of what appears to be the same stuff, extending around one entire chamber there. If it was gold instead of -- "

"Pyrites," supplied the Professor.

"Yes. It would make a man very rich, would it not?" asked Tad rising.

"Undoubtedly," smiled the Professor, bowing the boy out courteously.

Professor Zepplin, from the opening of his tent, watched Tad until the latter had joined his companions, after which he pulled the flap shut, quickly seating himself in front of his camp table.

Having done so, he proceeded to examine the two pieces of metal under a magnifying glass. Then with his geologist's hammer he broke off bits of the metal, through all of which sparkled the bright yellow particles.

The German got out his field kit, from which he selected several bottles with glass stoppers, arranging these on the table in front of him. This done, he pulverized a small quantity of the rock, with short, quick raps of the hammer, placing the powder thus made on a plate.

"One part nitric acid, two parts hydrochloric acid," he muttered, pouring the desired quantities from the bottles.

These preparations having been made, the Professor's next move was to apply a blowpipe to some of the metal from the pulverized ore, thus forming a small yellow button. This he dissolved in the aqua regia, formed by the combination of the two acids, and applied the usual chemical tests.

As he did so, Professor Zepplin's eyes glowed with a strange light.

He sprang up, peered cautiously from behind the tent flap, then settled himself once more to his experiments.

Again he went through a similar process with the powder made from still another chunk of the ore. The same result followed.

"Gold! Gold! Rich yellow gold!" breathed the scientist.

He sat with head bowed, breathing heavily, his fascinated gaze fixed on the shining metal.

"Can it be possible!" he murmured.

The loud laughter of the boys off by the camp fire was borne to his ears. But Professor Zepplin did not seem to hear the sounds. He was lost in deep thought.

# CHAPTER XVII

## THE PONIES STAMPEDE

Next morning the camp was stirring as the first gray streaks appeared on the eastern horizon.

Each saddle bag was quickly packed with hard tack, coffee and other necessaries which might be easily carried, the rest of the space being taken up with cartridges and the like. Blankets were rolled, ready to be strapped behind the saddles on the ponies' backs.

The luggage was to be reduced to the absolute needs of the party, but with the possibility of having to remain out over night, their requirements were greater than if they had intended to return the same evening.

Before they had finished their hurried breakfast, Ben Tackers appeared, accompanied by two vicious looking hounds, whose red eyes and beetle brows made the boys hesitate to approach them at first.

However, after the Pony Riders had tossed small chunks of cooked bear meat to them, the animals, by wagging their tails, showed that nothing need be feared from them.

No sooner were the guns brought out than the dogs,

beginning to understand what was in the air, bounded from one to another of the lads, barking and yelping with keen delight.

All was activity in the camp. Ponies were quickly rubbed down, saddled and bridled, blankets strapped on, and, at a command from Tad Butler, the young hunters fairly threw themselves into their saddles. The party moved off, with the enthusiastic riders waving their hats and shouting farewells to those who had been left behind.

Jose swung a dishpan, grinning broadly, while the Professor smiled and nodded at the departing horsemen. In a few moments the voices of the boys had become only a distant murmur.

"Come into my tent a moment, Mr. Tackers," invited the Professor.

The old mountaineer accepted the invitation apparently somewhat grudgingly.

"I hear considerable about gold being found in this neighborhood, occasionally, Mr. Tackers. What has been your experience, may I ask?"

"There's some as has found pay dirt," answered Ben. "But I reckon Ben Tackers don't bother his head about it."

"Hm-m-m-m," mused the Professor. "What is the nearest railroad station to this placet"

"Eagle Pass. 'Bout twenty miles from here, due east."

"How long would it take you to make the trip there and back?"

"Wouldn't make it again. Just been there. Haven't any horse."

"I have a horse, Mr. Tackers, and I should very much like to have you make this trip for me," announced the Professor, coming directly to the point. "I will pay you well for your trouble, but with the understanding that you say nothing of it to anyoue. The errand on which I am asking you to go is a confidential one. You will not mention it even to Lige Thomas. And, of course, it goes without saying that I do not wish the boys to know about it, either."

Ben peered at the Professor from behind his bushy eyebrows, with suspicion plainly written in his beady eyes.

"What for?" he grunted.

"That I cannot tell you - in fact it is not necessary for you to know. When you get there, all you will be required to do will be to hand two packages to the express agent there, with instructions to forward them at once to their destination, which will be Denver."

"What'll you give?"

"How much will you charge?" asked the Professor.

Ben considered for a moment.

"'Bout fifty cents, I reckon," he answered hesitatingly, as if thinking the amount named would be too much.

"I'll give you five times that," announced the Professor promptly.

"No; fifty cents 'll be 'bout right."

"How soon can you start?"

"Now, I reckon."

"Be ready in an hour, and I will have the packages for you. When will you return?"

"To-night."

"Good. Now he off and get yourself ready. You know where my horse is. And, by the way, I shall want you to make the trip again no later than the day after to-morrow, as I shall expect an answer to my message by that time. For that service I shall be glad to pay you the same."

"No; fifty cents will cover it all."

"Have it your own way."

Ben, understanding that the interview was at an end, rose and left the tent. Professor Zepplin then took one of the ore specimens from his pocket and packed it carefully in a small pasteboard box, wrapping and tying the package with great care.

Next, he wrote industriously for some twenty minutes. The letter he sealed in a large, tough envelope, after which he leaned back, lost in thought.

"Things couldn't be better," he muttered. Ben, upon his

return, received the packages which he was to express, and a few moments later had ridden from camp on old Bobtail, headed for Eagle Pass.

"I rather think I have turned a trick that will surprise some people," chuckled the Professor. "Perhaps I'll even surprise myself."

Later in the morning he strolled up to the cave entrance, hammer in hand, breaking off a bit of rock here and there, all of which he dropped into a little leathern bag that he carried attached to his belt. Yet the Professor wisely concluded not to take the chance of entering the cave alone, much as he wished to do so.

The young hunters, in the meantime, were plodding along on their ponies on their way to the hunting grounds, which lay some ten miles to the northward of their camp. They found rough traveling. Instead of following the ridges, they were now moving at right angles to them, which carried the boys over mountains, down through gulches and ravines, over narrow, dangerous passes and rocky slopes that they would not have believed it was possible for either man or horse to scale.

"Regular goats, these ponies," said Tad proudly. "Regular trick ponies, all of them."

"They have to be or break their necks," replied Walter.

"Or ours," added Ned Rector.

"I don't see any wild beasts, but I feel hungry," declared Stacy.

"My stomach tells me it's time for the 'chuck wagon,' as Lige Thomas calls it, to drive up."

"Tighten your belt - tighten your belt," jeered Ned. "Cheer up! You'll be hungrier bye-and-bye."

The boys munched their hard tack in the saddle, the guide being anxious to get, before nightfall, to the grounds where Tackers had advised him the bob-cats were plentiful. Already the dogs were lolling with tongues protruding from their mouths, not being used to running the trail in such warm weather. Now and then they would plunge into a cool mountain stream, immersing themselves to the tips of their noses where the water was deep enough, and sending up a shower of glistening spray as they shook themselves free of the water after springing to the bank again.

It was close to the hour of sunset when the guide finally gave the word to halt. Lige prepared the supper while the boys bathed and rubbed down their ponies, after which they busied themselves cutting boughs for their beds, which they now were well able to make without assistance from their guide.

Bronzed almost to a copper color, the lads were teeming with health and spirits. Even Walter Perkins, for the first time in his life, felt the red blood coursing healthfully through his veins, for he was fast hardening himself to the rough life of the mountains.

All were tired enough to seek their beds early. Wrapping themselves in their blankets, they were soon asleep.

Midnight came, and the camp fire slowly died away to

a dull, lurid pile of red hot coals that shed a flicker of light now and then, as some charred stick flamed up and was consumed. A long, weird, wailing cry, as of some human being in dire distress, broke on the stillness of the night.

The boys awoke with a start.

"What's that?" whispered Chunky, shivering in his bed.

"Nothing," growled Ned. "What did you wake me up for?"

Once more the thrilling cry woke the echoes, wailing from rock to rock, and gathering volume, until it seemed as if there were many voices instead of only one.

The ponies sprang to their feet with snorts of fear, while the boys, little less startled, leaped from their beds with blanching faces.

The guide was already on his feet, rifle in hand.

Again the cry was repeated, this time seeming to come from directly over their heads, somewhere up the rocky side of the gulch in which they were encamped.

Even horses trained to mountain work had been known to stampede under less provocation. The frightened ponies suddenly settled back on their haunches. There was a sound of breaking leather, as the straps with which they were tethered parted, and the little animals were free.

"Stop them! Stop them! Jump for them!" roared the guide.

But his warning command had come to late. With neighs of terror, the animals dashed straight through the camp, some leaping over the boys' cots as they went.

"Catch them!" thundered Lige. "It's a cougar stampeding them so he can catch them himself."

# CHAPTER XVIII

## ON A PERILOUS HIDE

"Grab him! Don't let him get by you!"

One of the ponies swept by Tad Butler like a black projectile. The boy's hand shot out, fastening itself in the pony's mane.

Tad's feet left the ground instantly, his body being jerked violently into the air, only to strike the earth again a rod further on. So rapidly was the pony moving, that the boy was unable to pull himself up sufficiently to mount it.

Almost in a twinkling Tad had been lifted out of the camp and whisked from the sight of his companions. The lad was taking what he realized to be the most perilous ride of his life.

As soon as he was able to get his breath, he began coaxing the pony, but the continual bobbing of his body against the side of the terrified animal outweighed the persuasive tones of his urging. With each bump, the little animal, with a frightened snort, would leap into the air and plunge ahead again.

Tad did not know to which of the ponies he was

clinging. Nor did he find an opportunity to satisfy himself on this point.

His flesh was torn from contact with thorns, while his face was ribbed from the whipping it had received by being dragged through the thick undergrowth, until tiny rivulets of blood trickled down his cheeks and neck.

Yet Tad Butler clung to the mane of the racing pony with desperate courage. He had not the slightest thought of letting go until ho should finally have subdued the animal.

"Whoa, Texas! Whoa, Jimmie! Whoa, Jo-Jo!" he soothed, trying the name of each of the ponies in turn. But it was all to no purpose. Finally, the little animal slackened its speed, somewhat, as it began the ascent of a steep rise of ground. Tad took instant advantage of the opportunity, and, after great effort, succeeded in throwing his right hand over the pony's back. Then his right leg was jerked up. It came down violently on the animal's rump.

Startled, the pony sprang forward once more, causing Tad to slide back to his former unpleasant position. But the boy had succeeded in getting a mane-hold with his right hand as well. This was a distinct gain, besides relieving the fearful strain on his left hand, the fingers of which were now cramped and numb. Hardly any sense of feeling remained in them. Instead of being dragged along on his left side, the plucky lad was now able, with great effort, to keep his face to the front.

"If I could only get my hand on his nose and pinch it now, I'd stop him," breathed Tad Butler.

In the meantime, excitement at the camp was at fever heat. Lige had failed to bring down the cougar and every one of the ponies had disappeared.

"Bring torches!" commanded the guide calmly, not wishing to let the boys see that he was in the least disturbed. "We must try to round up some of the stock. One of you build up the fire."

"But Tad?" urged Walter. "Don't you know Tad's gone? He'll be lost. We must go after him at once."

"That's what I want you to start the fire for - so he can see it. He'll come back with the pony. No fear about that, for Tad Butler is not the boy to give up until he has accomplished what he's set out to do. One of you must remain here, though, while the rest of us go out to look for the stock. Will you stay, Ned?"

"I will," answered the boy, though far from relishing the task assigned to him.

"You have your rifle. Signal us by shooting into the air if anything happens. But be careful. Don't get the 'buck fever' and let go at us, or at Tad, if he should return before we get back."

"I'll be careful," answered the boy. "Please don't worry about me. Any danger of that cougar jumping down on me here?" he asked, glancing apprehensively at the rocks overhead.

"I think not. He's gone. We shall be more likely to see him than you will. It's the ponies the brute's after. And he may have gotten one of them before this," added the guide.

Frank Gee Patchin

Ned pluckily took his station just outside the circle of light formed by the replenished fire, and sat down with rifle laid across his knees.

The guide, with Walter Perkins and Stacy Brown, set off at a trot in search of the stampeded ponies. At Lige's direction they spread out so as to cover as much ground as possible, the torches making it well nigh impossible for any of them to get lost.

"Call your ponies," advised the guide. "We may be able to pick up some of them in that way after they have spent themselves."

Yet, though the forest rang with their calls, no trace were they able to find of the missing animals.

"No use," announced Lige finally. "We shall only get lost ourselves. It will be better to return to camp and wait for daylight. If the cougar is going to eat any of them, he probably has them by this time. However, I think my shooting has frightened him off, and that he is several miles from here by now. That was my main object in wasting so much ammunition on the beast."

"Yes, but what are we going to do about Tad?" insisted Walter.

"If he has not returned, we can do nothing more than to keep the fire burning and discharge our guns now and then to let him know where we are. When daylight comes, I probably shall be able to follow his trail. But first of all we must get the ponies. We can do nothing without them."

"Do you think we ever shall find them?" asked Stacy.

"I most certainly hope so. At least, I expect to get some of them. If any are then missing, we can buy a couple at Eagle Pass, which is not very far. But you trust Master Tad to take care of himself. He'll get back somehow, My duty is to remain with you boys. We will look him up together when we get something to ride on."

The little band trudged ruefully through the dark forest on their return to camp, guided carefully by Lige, without whom they surely would have lost their way.

In the meantime, Tad had been dragged over an entire mountain range, the ranges in this case, however, being no more than a succession of summits of low peaks. The pony had reached the top of one of these when, without pausing in its mad course, it dashed on over the crest, and started down the opposite side.

All at once Tad realized that they were treading on thin air. The meaning of it all, smote him like a blow.

"We're over the cliff!" he groaned.

# CHAPTER XIX

## LOST IN THE MOUNTAINS

Fortunately, however, their fall proved to be a very short one, though to Tad it seemed as if they had been falling for an hour. Boy and horse landed on a soft, mossy bank, rolling over and over, the pony kicking and squealing with fear, until, finally, both came to a stop at the bottom of the hill.

Tad was unharmed, save for the unmerciful treatment he had received during his record-breaking journey. Yet, he proposed to take no further chances of losing his horse, if he had the good fortune to find the animal still alive. Tad came up like a rubber ball. With a quick leap, he threw himself fairly on the pony's side. The impact made the little horse grunt, his feet beating a tattoo in the air in his desperate struggles to free himself.

"Whoa!" commanded Tad sharply, sliding forward and sitting on the animal's head, which position he calmly maintained, until the pony, realizing the uselessness of further opposition, lay back conquered.

Yet the boy did not rise immediately. Instead, he patted the pony's neck gently, speaking soothing words and calming it until the animal's quivering muscles relaxed and it lay breathing naturally.

"Good boy, Jimmie," he said, recognizing the pony as Ned's. "Now, after you have rested a bit we'll see what we can do about getting back to camp. If I'm any judge, you and I are not going to have a very easy time of it on the back track, either, Jimmie."

Without a compass, with only a hazy idea of the direction in which they had been traveling, Tad's task indeed was a difficult one.

"I think we'll walk a bit, Jimmie," he confided to the pony, and, taking the little animal by the bridle, began leading it cautiously up the slope, which he ascended by a roundabout course, remembering the jump they had taken on the way down. Tad was not likely to forget that.

The boy's eyes were heavy for want of sleep and his wounds pained him beyoud words. After somewhat more than an hour's journey he pulled up, looking about him.

"I am afraid we two pards are lost, Jimmie."

The pony rubbed its nose against him as if in confirmation of the lad's words.

"And the further we go, the more we shall be lost. Jimmie, the best thing for you and me to do will be to go to bed. Lie down, Jimmie, that's a good boy."

As Tad tapped the pony gently on the knees the little animal slowly lowered himself to the ground, finally rolling over on his side with a snort.

"Good boy," soothed Tad. Then snuggling down, with the pony's neck for his pillow, the bridle rein twisted about one hand, Tad went as sound asleep as if he had not a care in the world, and without thought of the perils which the mountains about them held.

Yet some good fairy must have been watching over Tad Butler, for not a sound broke the stillness until a whinny from Jimmie at last disturbed his slumbers.

The boy opened his eyes in amazement. It was broad daylight.

Tad's first care was to tether the pony to a sapling, after which he searched about until he found a mountain stream, in which he washed, feeling greatly refreshed afterward. He then treated the pony as he had himself, washing the animal down, and allowing it to quench it's thirst in the stream.

"Not much of a breakfast, is it, Jimmie? But you can help yourself to leaves. That's where you have the best of me. Not being a horse, I can't eat leaves. I wonder where I am!"

Gazing about him inquiringly, the boy failed to recognize the landscape at all. In fact, he did not believe he ever had seen it before. When the sun rose he declared to himself that it had come right up out of the west. What little sense of direction he might have had left was entirely lost after this, and Tad sat down to think matters over.

Once he raised his head sharply and listened. He was sure that he had heard a shot, far off toward the rising sun.

Tad wished with all his heart, that he had his rifle with him, for he realized that with it he might be able to attract attention.

"I certainly cannot sit here and starve to death," he decided after Jimmie had satisfied his own hunger from the fresh green leaves. "Come on, Jimmie; we'll go somewhere, anyway.

Saying which, Tad methodically patched the broken bridle rein together, mounted the pony's bare back and set off to climb the low mountain that loomed ahead of him.

He had gone on thus for nearly two hours, without finding any trace of either the camp or his late companions, when a sound off in the bushes to the right of him caused him to pull Jimmie up sharply. Jimmie pricked up his ears and whinnied.

"That's strange," muttered Tad. "He wouldn't be likely to do that if it was a wild animal over there. Judging from past experiences, he'd run."

Once more did Jimmie set up a loud whinny, and to Tad's surprise and delight, the signal was answered by a similar call off in the sage brush.

"It's a horse. I believe it's one of the ponies," cried Tad, turning his mount in the direction from which the sounds had seemed to come, and galloping rapidly toward the place. Next, the boy uttered a shout of joy.

His delight was great, after he had penetrated the sage, to come suddenly upon a pony contentedly munching a mouthful of green leaves, and gazing at him with great wondering eyes.

"Texas!" shouted the boy.

Tad had indeed come upon his own faithful little pony.

"Texas, you rascal, you come right here. What do you mean by running away from me like this?"

Texas swished his tail, shaking his head and stamping his feet as if in mute protest at his owner's chiding.

Yet the pony made no attempt to run away as his master rode up beside him. Leaping to the ground, Tad petted the animal, throwing his arms about its neck, as if he had found a long lost friend. The two ponies, too, rubbed noses, and in other ways expressed their satisfaction at once more being together.

Now, reassured, and almost as well satisfied as if he had eaten a hearty breakfast, Tad mounted his own pony, and, taking Jimmie in tow, pressed on once more, hoping eventually to come out somewhere near the camp.

But the boy's companions had not been idle. Lige had prepared their breakfast without waking them. When he called them they sprang up, rubbing their eyes, and a few minutes later gathered around the hot meal.

"What is the first thing this morning?" asked Ned after learning that Tad had not yet returned.

"Breakfast," answered the guide. "Next, we'll look for the ponies, then go after Master Tad."

More fortunate in their search than they had hoped for, the party within the hour succeeded in rounding up all the ponies save Jimmie and Texas. One of the two they knew Tad had gone away with, so, after a council, it was decided to take the animals they had captured and make an effort to find Tad Butler.

"I'm going to try an experiment," announced Lige, after they had returned to camp with the stock.

Calling the hounds, Ginger and Mustard, to him, the guide allowed them to sniff the saddles and saddle cloths of Jimmie and Texas. After that, he showed them Tad Butler's hat.

The intelligent animals, after sniffing attentively at the articles, looked up at the guide as much as if to say: "Well, what about it?"

"Go after them! Fetch them, Ginger and Mustard!" he urged.

With noisy barks, the dogs began running about the camp with noses to the ground, sniffing at the ponies again and again, the little party in the meantime, watching them with keen interest.

All at once, with a deep bay, Mustard struck out for the bushes, followed an instant later by Ginger.

"They've got it! They've got it!" shouted Lige. "That's the way Tad went. Now, if those brutes don't get sidetracked on the trail of a bob-cat, we ought to round up some of our missing friends."

Lige bade Ned to accompany him on Jo-Jo, and

directed the others to remain in camp - not to move from it until their return. Then the two horsemen set off at a gallop, following the swiftly moving dogs.

Lige knew that he was on the right track, for Tad, as he was dragged through the bushes, had left a plainly marked trail - that is, plain to the experienced eyes of the mountain guide, who nodded his head with satisfaction as he noted the course the dogs were taking.

Tad pulled up his pony, and, leaning forward, listened intently.

He faintly caught the distant baying of a hound.

Placing a hand to his mouth, he gave a long, piercing war whoop.

The dogs' baying seemed to come nearer. Now and then, as the animals sank into a ravine, the sound would be lost momentarily, only to be taken up again with added force when the crest of the hill was reached.

Once more, Tad sent out his long, thrilling war-cry.

It was answered by a rifle shot, but from the perplexing echoes he was unable to place it. The ponies now pricked up their ears inquiringly. Jimmie snorted, and, for the moment, acted as if he were ready to bolt again. Tad slapped him smartly on the flanks, sternly commanding him to stand still.

"There they are!" cried the boy, as the dogs, stretched out to their full lengths, with tails held straight out behind them, swept down a gentle slope on the other side of the valley, and, taking the hill on his side, rose rapidly to the pinnacle where he was sitting on his pony.

"Ginger! Mustard!" was the glad cry uttered by Tad Butler, as the dogs, yelping with joy at the sound of his voice, came bounding to him, while the ponies reared and plunged in the excess of their excitement.

Tad leaped from his mount, petting and fondling the hounds, hugging them as they leaped upon him, and shouting at the top of his voice, as he heard still another shot on the other side of the hill.

A few moments later, he made out the figures of two horsemen on the opposite ridge, following on in the trail of the dogs. They were Ned Rector and the guide, Lige Thomas.

The two set up a glad shout as they made out Tad, waving his arms and gesticulating.

"Come on, doggies! It's breakfast for us, now!" cried Tad, leaping to Texas' back, leading Jimmie dashing down the hill to meet the oncoming horsemen.

"Hooray!" welcomed Ned Rector.

And amid the shouts of the boys and the barking of the dogs, rescuers and rescued drew swiftly toward each other.

Frank Gee Patchin

# CHAPTER XX

## THE DOGS TREE A CAT

Walter and Chunky finally made out Tad, tattered and torn, but riding his pony proudly, approaching the camp. It was a warm welcome that the two boys extended to the returning horsemen, after they had finally dismounted and staked down their ponies. The plucky lad was kept busy for some time telling them of his thrilling experience on the wild ride of the night before.

"And now, I guess we had better lay up for the day," decided the guide. "You must be pretty well tired out after your little trip. The rest of us didn't get much sleep last night, either."

"No," protested Tad. "I never was more fit in my life. I am crazy to start on our hunting trip."

"So are we," shouted the boys in chorus.

"All right, then. Pack up while Tad is getting something to eat. He must have a large-sized appetite by this time," smiled Lige Thomas.

"If I had a chunk of that bear meat that we got the other day, I'd show you what sort of an appetite I have," laughed Tad. "There's something about this mountain air that would lead a man to sell his blouse for a square meal. Where's my rifle?"

"Over there by your bunk," answered Walter. "You go ahead and eat. We'll pack the pony for you while you are breakfasting."

Tad did so, and an hour later the Pony Riders were once more in the saddle.

"I think I'll put the dogs on the trail of the fellow that upset our plans so thoroughly last night," decided Lige. "He probably is a long way from here by this time, but it will be a good trail to warm the hounds up on."

Bidding the boys draw down the valley half a mile or so, where he said he would join them, Lige went in the opposite direction, and, picking his way along a ledge, sent the dogs on ahead of him. The hounds soon scented the trail, though on the bare rocks they had considerable difficulty in picking it up.

After watching them for a few moments, Lige urged them out into the brush, where he thought the scent might be more marked. His judgment was verified when, a moment later, a yelp from Mustard told him the faithful animal had picked up the trail at last.

Turning back, the guide hastened to the foot of the mountain, whence he galloped down the valley to join the boys, who, having heard the deep baying of the hounds, were restless to be off.

"What are they doing?" called Walter, observing Lige approaching.

"They're after the cougar. Set your horses at a gallop."

The Pony Riders needed no urging, for they were keen for the excitement of the chase. The hounds, by this time, had obtained quite a lead on them, though the boys still could hear their hoarse voices.

"They are following the ridge yet," decided Lige. "The fellow ought to cross over pretty soon. I think if we will turn to the left, here, and climb the mountain, we may be able to save some distance. But don't speak to the dogs if they pass anywhere near you. It might throw them off the scent."

Half an hour after they had turned off, they were rewarded by seeing the dogs racing down the opposite hill, in great leaps and bounds, crossing the valley a short quarter of a mile ahead of the party.

The ponies, which had been walking since they turned off, were now sent forward at a slow gallop again, soon falling in close behind the hounds.

"They've got him!" cried Lige.

"Got who?" asked Chunky.

"I don't know. The cougar, I presume. Don't you hear them?"

"I hear the dogs barking, that's all," replied Ned.

"And I hear more than that," said the guide, with a peculiar smile. "Don't you distinguish a difference in the tone of one of the dogs' bark?"

"No, I don't," snapped Chunky. "All barks sound alike to me."

"Mustard is baying 'treed,'" said the guide. "Hurry, if you want to be in at the death. If you don't the dogs either will kill him or get killed before we can reach them."

Putting spurs to their mounts, the hunters set off at a livelier gallop, and soon the deep tones of the hounds began to grow louder. Now, too, the boys were able to catch a new note - a note almost of triumph, it seemed to them, in the dogs' hoarse baying.

"Stick to your ponies. Don't leave them. If it's a cougar, he is liable to stampede them again. And don't any of you shoot until I give you the word."

"There he is!" cried Tad, pointing to a low-spreading pinyon tree. "I can see him moving around in the top there. May I take a shot at him, Mr. Thomas?"

"No; do you want to kill the dogs?"

"The dogs?"

"Certainly. That is one of the dogs up there. Probably Mustard," said the guide.

"What's that? Dogs climb trees?" demanded Chunky, laughing uproariously.

"Keep still! Do you want to spoil our fun?" growled Ned.

"The idea! Dogs climb trees!" And Chunky Brown

went off into a paroxysm of silent mirth, his rotund body convulsed with merriment.

"Mustard can climb a tree as well as you can, if not better," answered Lige sharply. "Use your eyes, and you will see for yourself. That is one of the dogs that you see in the tree there - not a cougar. Ah! There goes the other one!" he cried, pointing with his rifle.

And, sure enough, it was.

"It's Ginger!" exclaimed Walter in amazement.

The hound was creeping cautiously up the sloping trunk of the spreading tree, following in the wake of his companion, whose presence in the tree was indicated only by the movement of the slender limbs which he fastened upon to keep from losing his balance.

"What are they after?' asked Ned. "Perhaps a cougar. I can't tell, yet," replied the guide, keeping his eye fixed on the tree.

A yelp of pain and anger followed close upon his words, and a dark object came plunging from the tree.

"There goes one of the dogs!" shouted Lige. "That's too bad."

The hound had approached too close to the animal in the tree, and a mighty paw had smitten it fairly on the nose, hurling it violently to the ground.

Mustard, nothing daunted, scrambled to his feet with an angry roar, the blood trickling from his injured nose, and pluckily began digging his claws into the bark of the pinyon tree, up which he slowly pulled himself again.

"Well, if that doesn't beat all!" marveled Chunky. "He is climbing that tree!"

"He surely is," agreed Walter, his eyes fairly bulging with surprise at the unusual spectacle. "And there's the other one away up in the top there. Why doesn't he fall off?"

"He prefers to remain up a tree, I imagine," laughed Ned Rector, without withdrawing his gaze from the unusual exhibition.

A squall of rage from the tree top caused the boys to draw their reins tighter, the ponies champing at their bits and pawing restlessly. The ugly sound thrilled the lads through and through. The deep, menacing growl of the dog that was crawling up the sloping trunk voiced his anxiety to take part in the desperate battle that was being waged above them.

"Ginger's got hold of him!" shouted the guide.

"Got hold of who?" demanded Chunky.

"You'll see in a minute," growled Ned.

"Look out! There he comes!" came the warning voice of the guide. "Back, out of the way!"

From the dense foliage, as if suddenly projected from a great bow, leaped the curving body of the animal that the dogs had been harassing.

With a snarl of rage it landed lightly, almost at the feet of the assembled Pony Riders.

Stacy chanced to be nearest to the spot where the beast struck the ground. As it did so, his pony rose suddenly into the air. The boy, so intently watching the battle, had carelessly allowed his reins to drop from his hand to the neck of his mount.

"I'm going to fall off!" yelled Stacy, grabbing frantically for the pommel of his saddle.

He missed the pommel and slipped from the leather. Striking the smooth back of the horse, he tobogganed down and over the pony's rump in a flash, sitting down on the ground with a suddenness that caused him to utter a loud "Ouch!"

"He-help!" gasped the boy.

Before the snorting pony's fore feet had touched the earth. Tad made a grab for the bit, and was jerked from his own pony as a result. But still he clung doggedly to his own bridle rein with one hand, hanging to the other plunging animal with the other.

The others of the party were having all they could do to manage their own horses, and hence were unable to offer Tad any assistance at that moment. So mixed in the melee of flying hoofs and plunging bodies was Tad Butler, that for a few seconds the onlookers were quite unable to tell which was pony and which was boy.

Yet the lad was amply able to fight his own battles, and he was doing so with a grim determination that knew not failure. The ponies already were lessening their frantic efforts to get away.

"It's a bob-cat!" shouted Lige, as soon as he had succeeded in swinging his horse about so he could get a good view of the animal, which was now bounding away.

Throwing his rifle to his shoulder, the guide took a snap shot at the fleeing cat, which now was no more than an undulating black streak. His bullet kicked up a little cloud of dirt just behind the bob-cat, which served only to hasten its pace. A moment more and the little animal had plunged head first into a depression in the ground and quickly crawled into a hole, probably its home.

"Too bad," groaned Ned Rector. "Now, we've lost him."

"Never mind," soothed Lige. "There are more of them in the mountains. Besides, it's a good experience for you, before we tackle bigger game. We'll see if we can't bag a cat before the day is over."

Chunky pulled himself up ruefully, rubbing his body and pinching himself to make sure that no serious damage had been done. Satisfying himself on this point, he straightened up, gazing from one to the other of his companions pityingly.

"You fellows make me weary," he growled.

"The whole bunch of you can't do with guns what I did with a little stick. Gimme my pony."

"It occurs to me," retorted Tad, after having subdued

the ponies, "that you weren't doing much of anything, either. If I remember correctly, you were sitting on the ground during most of the circus."

# CHAPTER XXI

## A COUGAR AT BAY

The dogs did not succeed in picking up another trail that day, so, late in the afternoon, the guide directed them to make camp by a stream, under the tall, clustering spruces in a deep ravine.

Tired from their hard run, the hounds threw themselves down by the cool stream to satisfy their thirst. Mustard employed his time in licking his wounded nose, where the claws of the bob-cat had raked it. Altogether the two animals appeared more disappointed over the loss of their quarry than did the boys themselves. While responding to the caresses of their young masters, the dogs were irritable to the point of snapping angrily at each other whenever they approached one another close enough to do so.

"They don't seem to enjoy each other's company," said Stacy, observing the animals curiously.

"They're always that way after a chase," answered the guide. "They will be friendly to their masters, but extremely irritable to each other. By to-morrow morning the hounds will be bosom friends, you will find."

"Humph! I wouldn't like to belong to that family," decided Chunky.

Next morning, Lige decided that it would he best to move further north for cougar, they having failed to strike the trail of any on the previous day. Somehow, the dogs had lost the trail of the one that had so recently disturbed the camp, picking up the scent of the bob-cat instead.

This frequently was the case, as the guide informed them while they were riding along in the fresh morning air. The dogs had not been freed yet, Lige leading them along by the side of his pony on a long leash.

Tad was trailing along a few rods to the rear. A sudden exclamation from him caused the others to pull up sharply.

The lad's eyes were fixed on a tree a short distance ahead of him beneath which the party had just passed.

"What is it?" demanded Lige in a low voice.

As if in answer to his question, the hounds uttered a deep, menacing growl.

Tad made no reply, but signaled with his hand that they were to remain quietly where they were.

They saw him slip off the strap that held the rifle to his back and bring the weapon around in front of him. There he paused, holding the gun idly in one hand, his gaze still fixed on the top of the tree.

All at once the butt of the rifle leaped to his shoulder.

There was a puff of smoke, a crash, followed by a loud squall, and a great floundering about among the branches.

Without lowering the weapon from his shoulder, the young hunter let go another shot.

The squalling ceased suddenly, but the disturbance in the tree continued, sounding as if some heavy body were falling through the branches.

This proved to be the case. In a moment more the animal he had fired at came tumbling down, landing in a quivering heap at the foot of the tree.

Tad lowered the muzzle of his smoking weapon, gazing in keen satisfaction at the victim of his successful shot.

"Good shot!" glowed Lige. "It's a cat." Yet, before he could dismount, the hounds had wrenched themselves free and pounced upon the body of the dead bob-cat. With savage growls they tore the sleek hide into ribbons, on one side, and were devouring the flesh of the animal ravenously.

The hide was ruined.

"Let them alone!" ordered Lige. "That's the only fun they get out of the game. They'll be keen to get on the track of a cougar, now that they have tasted blood." And so it proved.

With their first big game, on this trip, at their feet, the boys were eager to be off for the haunts of the cruel cougar. To their disappointment, however, they were able to sight nothing more interesting than a gaunt gray wolf, at which Ned took a long shot and missed.

"Might as well try to hit a razor's edge at that distance," said Lige. "They have no flesh on them at all, to speak of, now -- "

"Will they bite?" asked Chunky innocently. "A pack of them would eat you, bones and all, in a few moments," grinned Lige.

Chunky shuddered.

"But the gray wolf, when taken young, makes an ideal pet. Some of the best cougar hounds I nave ever seen were trained wolves, working with a pack of regular hounds, of course," he explained. Leaving the carcass of the bob-oat for the ravens and magpies, which were already hovering about in the tall trees awaiting their turn at it, the hunters moved on.

No other game being found that day, the party turned eastward, where camp was made, this time on the flat top of a low-lying mountain. Nor was it until late the following afternoon that the dogs appeared to have struck a promising lead. From the way they worked Lige thought they were trailing a black bear.

Forcing the ponies into a brisk trot, the boys still found themselves falling behind the hounds. Then, at the guide's suggestion, they went in chase at a lively gallop.

The run continued for somewhat more than two hours, until the ponies began to lag, and until every bone in the bodies of the hunters seemed to be crying aloud for rest. The going had been rougher than any they had yet experienced.

Now they found themselves in a country differing materially from any they had yet explored. The hills were lower and thickly studded with trees, the whole resembling an exaggerated rolling prairie.

"They've got him this time," announced the guide.

"Got what?" demanded Chunky.

"We'll know soon," answered Lige directing the boys to urge their ponies along, and at a rapid pace they came up with the hounds some twenty minutes later.

They were fighting some animal in a dense copse. It was a dinful racket they made in their desperate battle.

"It's a cougar," explained Lige. "No cat would make such a rumpus. Look out for yourselves. I guess you had better lead the ponies off to the right, there, and stake them securely, for we may have a fight on our own hook before we have finished here. Hurry if you want to see the fun."

The boys were back in a twinkling.

"Fix them so they can't get away?"

"Yes."

"Then all of you line up here on this side so we won't be shooting each other when the brute makes his attempt at a get-away, as he surely will, when the dogs give him a chance. Two of them can't hold him long.

We ought to have a pack."

They could hear the battle waging desperately in the bushes, which were being rapidly trampled down by the dogs and their victim, amid screams of rage from the animal and menacing, deadly growls from the hounds.

Soon the young hunters were able to make out the combatants, as the beast worked its way little by little to its right in an effort to get within reaching distance of a tree that it espied near by. But the dogs fought valiantly to outwit this very move.

"We've got a cougar this time!" shouted Lige triumphantly. "Look out for him!"

They could see the fighters plainly now. It was dangerous to fire for fear of hitting the hounds. Already they were bleeding where the fangs or claws of the ugly beast had raked them.

However, the dogs were working with keen intelligence. One would nip at a flank while the other played for the head of the cougar, in hopes of getting an opening.

Snarling, pawing, grinning, its ugly yellow teeth showing in two glistening rows, the beast fought savagely for its life.

Despite the guide's warning, Tad Butler and Ned Rector had drawn closer that they might get a better view of the sanguinary conflict.

"I'm afraid they'll never make it," groaned Lige. "It's

fearful odds. Everybody stand ready to let him have it when he breaks away. But keep cool. And be careful that you don't hit the dogs. Might better let the cat get away. There he goes!"

The huge beast leaped clear of the pocket into which the dogs had backed him.

"Don't shoot!" ordered the guide, observing one of the boys swinging his rifle down on the struggling animals.

As the big cat leaped, Mustard fastened his fangs into the beast's left leg, and was carried along with the cougar in its mighty spring. They could hear the hones grind as the iron jaws of the hound shut down on them.

With a scream of rage, the maddened animal came to a sudden stop. Its cruel yellow head shot out, jaws wide apart, aimed straight for Mustard, who was still hanging with desperate courage to the beast's leg.

Yet the momentary hesitation, the few seconds lost in stopping in its rapid flight and reaching back for Mustard, proved the cougar's undoing.

With a snarl that sent a shiver up and down the backs of the Pony Riders, Ginger threw himself at the head of the beast. The hound's powerful jaws closed upon it with a snap.

Over and over rolled the combatants, the dogs without a sound - the cougar uttering muffled screams, its great paws beating the air. One stroke reached Mustard, hurling him fully a rod away, where he fell and lay quivering, a dull red rent appearing in his glossy coat.

Frank Gee Patchin

The cougar, in an effort to throw Ginger off, was shaking his head, as a terrier would in killing a rat.

"Ah! He can't make it," cried Lige.

"Hang on, Ginger! Go it, Ginger!" encouraged the boys, now wild with excitement.

But the hound was fast losing his hold, and the hunters groaned in sympathy with him as they observed this.

Mustard, understanding this too, perhaps, struggled to his feet and staggered into the arena to assist his mate, only to meet a repetition of the calamity that had befallen him a few minutes before. Ginger's hold was broken at last. One great paw felled him to earth, and the cougar's yawning jaws closed over his head with crushing force.

Tad Butler's blood was coursing through his veins madly. He could endure it no longer. A second or so more and the faithful dog's life would be at an end. With a cry of warning to the others not to shoot, Tad leaped into the fray, Mustard, at the same time, hurling himself at the beast's throat, where he fastened and clung.

As Tad sprang forward, his hunting knife flashed from its sheath, and with a movement so quick that the eyes of the spectators failed to catch it, the boy drove the keen blade into the cougar's body, just back of the right shoulder.

At that instant the beast succeeded in freeing itself from the weakened hounds, and, straightening up with a frightful roar, leaped into the air, one huge paw catching Tad Butler and hurling him to the ground.

Tad shuddered convulsively, then lay still.

Lige Thomas's rifle roared out a hoarse protest, and at the end of its leap the cougar lurched forward and fell dead.

# CHAPTEE XXII

## PROFESSOR ZEPPLIN'S MYSTERIOUS FOE

Though Tad Butler had received an ugly wound where the sharp claw of the dying cougar had raked him from his right shoulder almost down to the waist line, his youthful vitality enabled him to throw off the shock of it in a very short time.

Making sure that the beast was dead, Lige rushed to the boy's side, and turning him over, made a hasty examination of his wounds.

Tad was unconscious.

"Is - is he dead?" breathed Walter, peering down into the pale face of his friend.

"No. He's alive, but he's had a mighty close call," answered Lige in a relieved tone, and each of the boys muttered a prayer of thankfulness.

"Bring me some water at once," commanded the guide.

Ned rushed away, returning in a few moments with his sombrero filled. In his excitement he dropped the hat in attempting to pass it to the guide, deluging the unconscious Tad with the cold water. Tad gasped and coughed, a liberal supply of the water having gone down hist throat.

"Clumsy!" growled Lige. "Get some more, but don't let go till I get hold of the hat this time."

By the time Ned had returned with the second hatful, Tad Butler was regaining consciousness, and in a few moments they had him sitting up.

The guide washed the boy's wound, and, laying on a covering of leaves, which he secured with adhesive plaster, allowed him to stand up.

"Well, young man, how do you feel?" he asked, with a grin.

"I feel sore. Did he bite me?"

"Luckily for you, he didn't. If you are going in for hand-to-hand mix-ups I'm afraid we shall have to leave off hunting. Old and experienced hunters have done what you did, but I must say it's the first time I ever heard of a boy even attempting it."

"Are the dogs dead?" asked Tad solicitously.

"No. But, like you, they're pretty sore. You saved Ginger's life, and I guess he knows it. You can see how he keeps crawling up to you, though he can hardly drag his body along."

"Good Ginger," soothed Tad, patting the wounded beast, which the hound acknowledged by a feeble wag of its tail.

"Now, if you boys are satisfied, I propose that we start back in the morning," advised Lige. "It will take us well into the second day to reach camp, and we may pick up some game on the way back. I'll skin the cat to-night after supper, so we can take the hide back with us. I guess you'll all agree that it belongs to Tad Butler?" smiled Lige.

"Well, I should say it does," returned Ned earnestly. "But he's welcome to it. If that's the way they get cougar skins, I'll roam through life without one, and be perfectly contented with my lot."

"Not many fellows would risk their lives for a dog," added Walter, with glowing eyes.

While the boys had been having such exciting times, Professor Zepplin also had been enjoying the delights of the mountains, as well as experiencing some of their more unpleasant features.

The lure of the yellow metal had gotten into the Professor's veins, immediately he had proved to his own satisfaction that that which Tad had discovered was real gold. The German could scarcely restrain his anxiety until the final return of Ben Tackers with the reply to the message he had sent on to Denver.

Ben had made the trip to Eagle Pass again on the third day, returning some time in the night, so that the Professor did not see him until the following day.

In the meantime, Professor Zepplin had not been idle. He had made frequent trips to the vicinity of the cave, bringing away with him each time a bagful of the ore, which he had detached with his hammer and chisel, all of which he had submitted to the blow-pipe, acid tests, and, in most instances, with the same result that had followed his first attempt.

The Professor's enthusiasm now was almost too great for his self-restraint. There could be no doubt of the correctness of his conclusions. There must be a rich vein of ore running through the rocks, terminating, he believed, in the cave itself.

Finally, urged on by this same enthusiasm, Professor Zepplin ventured in as far as the first chamber one afternoon, and what he found there raised his hopes to the highest pitch.

"I must be careful. I must be cautious. No one must know of my discovery just yet," he breathed, glancing apprehensively about, as he emerged from the cave on hands and knees.

Yet, as he came out, the Professor failed to observe two pairs of eyes that were watching his every movement from the rocks above the entrance to the cave.

Believing himself entirely alone, the Professor spread the ore he had just gathered on the ground before him, taking up each piece of mineral, fondling it and gazing upon it with glowing eyes.

"Gold! Bright yellow gold! A fortune, indeed!"

With a deep sigh of satisfaction, he gathered up the specimens, replacing them in his bag with great care. He drew the mouth of the bag shut, tying it securely.

So thoroughly absorbed was he with his great discovery, that he was all unconscious of the fact that a man had been creeping up to him from the rear while he had been thus engaged.

In one hand the fellow carried a stout stick, the free hand being employed to aid him in his cat-like creeping movements.

"I wonder if anyoue suspects," mused the scientist, sitting with a far-away look in his eyes. "Well, we shall see. We shall -- "

The words died on the Professor's lips, as the tough stick, which had been raised above him, was brought down with a resounding whack, squarely on the top of his uncovered head.

Sudden darkness overwhelmed Professor Zepplin. He sank down with a moan, into utter oblivion.

When finally his heavy eyelids had struggled apart, night had fallen. At first, he could not imagine where he was nor what had happened. Shooting pains throbbed through his head and down into his arms and body.

The Professor uttered a suppressed moan, closed his eyes and lay back, vainly groping about in his disordered mind for a solution of the mystery.

Step by step he went back over the occurrences of the afternoon, which gradually became clearer, until at last he reached the point where he had finished his examination of the specimens of ore, in front of the cave entrance.

"And that's where I am now," decided Professor Zepplin, sitting up. "But, what happened then? I have it. Something hit me."

His hand instinctively went to his injured head. Then, with trembling fingers he began searching for the bag of minerals.

It was nowhere to be found. The Professor marveled at this for some minutes.

Like a blow, the answer came to him.

"Robbed!" he exclaimed.

Struggling to his feet, the German staggered down the rocks toward the camp, calling for Jose with the full strength of his voice. The Professor having been assisted to his tent and a lotion prepared for his aching head, Jose was hurried off to the cabin of Ben Tackers with an urgent demand for his presence.

When Ben responded, and had listened to the full account of Professor Zepplin's mishap, he sat grave and thoughtful.

"Bad lot," he growled. "Ab Durkin's one of the most lawless critters on the Park Range; and I've got all I'm goin' to stand from him. The sheriff will settle him when he gits here -- "

"I don't care anything about the sheriff. The coward shall suffer for this, if he is the one who attacked me. I'll drive him out myself, if ou won't help me. I'll -- "

"I'm with you all right, pardner."

"Then, come. I'm ready now," urged the Professor rising.

"What you going to do?" "I am going back there to take possession of that claim. That's what I am going to do. And it will be worse for the man who tries to stop me," declared Professor Zepplin, taking a revolver from his kit, and examining it to see that all the chambers were loaded. "I'd like to see this man, Ab, attempt to interfere with my rights - I mean, interfere again."

Yet, had he known what was in store for him, the Professor might have hesitated before taking the step that he had determined upon.

# CHAPTER XXIII

## THE PONY RIDERS UNDER FIRE

With many a whoop and hurrah, the boys dashed into the home camp in the early forenoon of the following day.

Lige had left them three miles down the trail, that he might make a short cut to Eagle Pass for the purpose of getting word to the parents of the boys, that their trip had been concluded, and asking that directions for their further journeys might be sent to them at Denver, where they were to travel by easy stages.

The trail to camp being clear and easily followed, he felt no apprehension in allowing them to go on alone.

"Halloo the camp!" shouted Ned, hurling his sombrero on high, riding under and deftly catching it as it descended.

"Why, there's no one here!" exclaimed Tad Butler, looking about inquiringly, as they rode in.

Walter swung from his pony, and, hurrying to the tents, glanced into each in turn.

"That's queer. Looks as if no one had been here in a

Frank Gee Patchin

month. Well, suppose we unpack and wait."

"Somebody has been through these tents in a hurry," declared Tad after having made a hasty examination on his own account. "Did you notice that everything in the Professor's tent had been fairly turned inside out? There are our bows and arrows lying out there near where the camp fire was."

Now, the boys began to feel real concern.

"Tether the ponies and we will go out and see if we can find them," commanded Tad Butler.

"Shall we take our guns?" asked Stacy.

"Better not. Take your bows and arrows if you wish. We are going on the trail of two-footed game now, and we do not want to have guns. We might use them and be sorry for it afterwards."

Realizing the wisdom of his words, the boys laid aside their rifles, grabbed up their bows and quivers, and following Tad, who immediately struck off in the direction of the cave. Tad's own experience there was still fresh in memory.

At the entrance, they halted.

"Look at that! What do you think of that?" exclaimed Tad.

Above the entrance to the cave hung suspended a broad strip of sheeting. On it had been scrawled, evidently with a piece of blunt lead, the words:

THIS CLAIM BELONGS TO AB DURKIN. KEEP OFF!

The boys gazed at each other in amazement.

"We'll find out whom this claim belongs to!" declared Tad sternly. "I don't believe what that notice says at all. There is something more to this than we know about. Who'll go into the cave with me?"

"I will," chorused the boys.

"Follow me, then."

Tad moved forward, with the rest of the boys following closely behind him. But, as they started, a revolver shot rang out and a bullet sang by the head of Tad Butler.

"Back to the rocks!" shouted the boy, springing from the open place where they had been standing, at the same time urging his companions forward.

"What does this mean?" demanded Ned Rector.

"I don't know. We are in for trouble. Spread out and hide behind the boulders as well as you can, while we crawl back to camp. Chunky, you run for Ben Tackers as fast as your fat legs will carry you!"

With more order than might reasonably have been expected under the circumstances, the boys retreated rapidly, two more shots zipping over their heads as they leaped over a projecting ledge and scurried to cover without losing any time.

"I guess they're trying to scare us, that's all," decided Ned.

They could hear their unseen enemies, clambering down the rough ground that lay on either side of the cave, evidently bent on following them, now and then sending a bullet at one or the other of the dodging figures of the Pony Riders.

"Humph! Looks like it, doesn't it?" snapped Tad.

Suddenly rising to his full height, the boy waved his sombrero and hailed the men who bad been firing at them.

"Hold on, there! What are you trying to do? You're shooting at us! You had best look out what you are doing, unless you want to got into trouble yourselves. I -- "

The answer came promptly.

A gun barked viciously, and the plucky lad's sombrero was snipped from his hand, with a bullet hole through its broad brim.

Tad ducked behind a rock with amazing quickness.

"Spread out a little more, fellows. It won't he so easy to hit us," he commanded. "Walter, you watch out on either side of us, while Ned and I take care of the front."

"Wish I had my rifle. I'd show them," growled Ned.

"I don't," snapped Tad. "We've got trouble enough as it is."

The boys had been carrying on their conversation in low tones, that they might not betray their positions to their enemies.

"Get out of there, you young cubs!" suddenly roared a voice, whose owner they could not see. "I'll l'arn ye to interfere with other folks' business. I'll give yer five minutes to shake ther dust of this hy'ar mounting off yer feet. If any of ye is here then, it'll be the worse for ye. This claim belongs to Ab Durkin. Now, mosey! D'ye hear?"

Tad Butler did hear. And now he saw as well as heard.

Ab, confident that he had nothing to fear from the boys, had taken his station on a large boulder, from which position he was giving his orders to the Pony Riders. Tad, peering from behind the rock where he had taken refuge, saw an evil face, topped by a weather-worn sombrero, and, beyoud it, the figures of four other men whose faces he was unable to make out.

"I say, will ye git?"

"No!" shouted Tad, his face flushing, as all the old fighting spirit in him came to the surface.

"Then, take the consequences!"

Ab Durkin raised his revolver, peering from rock to rock, not certain now as to the exact location of the boys. He seemed ready to fire the instant he made out the mark he was seeking.

Tad Butler never had been more cool in his life, and a strange sense of elation possessed him.

Motioning to the boys to lie low, Tad fitted an arrow to his bow, after which he waited a few seconds, keenly watching the enemy and measuring the distance to him, with critical eyes.

All at once the boy's right arm drew back. There followed a sharp twang.

"Ouch!"

The mountaineer leaped straight up into the air, which action was followed by two shots in quick succession, as both of the man's revolvers were accidentally discharged, the bullets burying themselves harmlessly in the ground in front of him.

Tad's arrow had sped home. Its blunt end had been driven with powerful force, straight against the left ear of Ab Durkin, having been deflected slightly from where Tad had intended to plant it.

"Lie low!" commanded the boy.

The next instant, a shower of revolver shots flattened themselves against the rocks all about the boys.

"Give them a volley and drop back quickly!" ordered Tad.

Three bows twanged, and yells of rage told the boys that at least some of their missiles had gone home. This was a different sort of warfare from anything to which these mountaineers had been accustomed, and, somehow, it had begun to get on their nerves, desperate men though they were.

"Follow me. We must change our positions again. They've got our range now," directed Tad, and the boys, wriggling along on their stomachs, to the left, dutifully followed their leader.

Tad was heading for a clump of sage brush, so that their operations might be the better masked. While he was doing so, the mountaineers, who also had taken to cover, were bombarding the rocks from which the Pony Riders had just made their escape.

From their new position the boys were overjoyed to find that their enemies were in plain view.

"Take careful aim, and when I count three, let go at them. See that not one of you misses," directed the leader.

"Ready, now! One, two, three!"

Three bowstrings sang, and as many mountaineers, with yells of rage, began shooting, fanning every rock and bush about them, in hopes of driving from cover their tantalizing opponents.

At first they were at a loss to locate the boys' new position, but, after a little, as the arrows kept coming persistently from the sage bush, the mountaineers' bullets began to snip the leaves over the heads of the Pony Riders.

"Shoot slowly, and make every shot count!" directed Tad with stern emphasis.

Once, a bullet grazed Tad's left cheek, and Ned Rector narrowly missed death, escaping with the loss of a lock of hair. With rare generalship, Tad continually changed their positions, which tactics also were followed by the mountaineers, all the time crowding the boys nearer and nearer to their own camp.

Chunky had not yet returned, and Tad devoutly hoped that the boy would not be rash enough to attempt to do so now.

If anything, the boys thus far had the best of the battle, and although none had sustained a serious wound, every one of the mountaineers had marks on his body to show where blunt tipped arrows, driven by a strong arm, had been stopped.

Now, a new danger menaced the brave little band. Their quivers were nearly empty. Tad, discovering it, drew his hunting knife from its sheath, tossing it to Walter Perkins.

"Quick! Cut some sticks and make some arrows. Don't lose a second. Make them as straight as possible, or we shall be unable to hit a thing."

By the time their supply had become almost exhausted, Walter had succeeded in turning out more than half a dozen new arrows. Yet no sooner had they begun driving these at their enemies than the mountaineers sent up a yell of defiance. They recognized the predicament the boys were in.

"Cease firing!" commanded Tad, realizing at once that their enemies had discovered their plight.

"Fellows, we are about at the end of our rope. Give me the arrows. Then, you two make your get-away. But be careful not to expose your bodies to the fire of those brutes. When you get far enough away run for Ben Tackers' cabin. You can hide there, anyway," directed Tad Butler.

"Yes, but what are you going to do? You surely don't intend to remain here?" protested Walter.

"I'm going to cover your retreat. They'll think we have no more ammunition left and then they'll start to rush us. That's the time I'll surprise them. We have a few arrows left. They won't be so fast to -- "

"See here, Tad Butler, what do you take us for?" demanded Walter, his eyes snapping. "Do you think we are going to desert you and leave you here, perhaps to he killed?"

"While we run away?" added Ned. "I guess not. What breed of tenderfoot do you think we belong to?"

"No! We stay with you," announced Walter firmly.

"Oh, very well. I'm sorry. Hold your arrows till you have to shoot, but it would he much better for you to go while you have a chance."

Recognizing the helplessness of the boys, the mountaineers began moving on their position, revolver shots occasionally zipping against the rocks. It was almost impossible for the boys to return the fire with their few remaining arrows, for fear of exposing themselves to too great danger.

"I guess it's about up with us," said Tad, coolly stringing his last arrow.

# CHAPTER XXIII

## CONCLUSION

The faces of the three boys were pale, though a half smile played about the lips of Tad Butler. "Lie down!" he said.

Tad was watching the enemy from behind a rock, nervously fingering the arrow that lay across his bow.

At last the men had approached to within three or four rods of them. Tad rose, not a muscle of his body appearing to quiver when they sent a few shots at him.

Deliberately drawing back his bowstring, the boy drove one of the heavy missiles that Walter had cut for him full into the evil face of Ab Durkin. They could hear the impact as the heavy stick landed.

Ab toppled over backwards with a yell of rage.

"That's our last shot." Tad threw down his bow, standing with folded arms calmly facing the enemy. "Hands up!" rang the stern command. At first, Tad thought the order was directed at himself. Then a puzzling expression settled over his face as he saw the mountaineers suddenly wheel, then throw their hands above their heads.

Frank Gee Patchin

Lige Thomas, on his way to the Pass, had not gone far before he came up with the sheriff, to whom he explained what he had heard about the doings of Ab Durkin and his gang. While they were conversing, the sound of the shooting was borne faintly to them on the clear mountain air.

Suspecting something of the truth, Lige had wheeled his horse and ridden back with all speed, followed by the sheriff and his little posse. They had arrived at the moment when they were, perhaps, needed most.

Creeping down into an advantageous position, they had put a quick and sudden end to the onslaught of the mountaineers, who were in no mood for trifling with their young opponents now.

In a few moments the sheriff had each of the five men in handcuffs, and without having had to fire a shot. Tad, who had rushed out, followed by his companions, explained to the posse that the Professor and Jose were missing. He believed now that they were prisoners in the cave.

And there they found them - Professor Zepplin, Ben Tackers and Jose, bound hand and foot.

All of them bad been taken captive by the mountaineers when they visited the cave the night before.

Ab Durkin was fuming with rage.

"These cayuses was stealin' my claim," he snarled. "Understand me, they was stealin' the gold, and, when I tried to drive them off, they sailed into us -- "

"Yes, I observed that you were shooting at three boys," retorted the sheriff, sarcastically.

"See, thar's my mark over that hole in the ground," continued Ab pointing to the sign that was flapping idly in the breeze. "That's my claim and no man ain't goin' ter take it away from me, neither."

"My friend," retorted Professor Zepplin, stepping forward frowning. "If I did what you deserve, I should send a bullet into your miserable carcass. Instead I'm going to tell you about a little paper I have here."

All eyes instantly were centered on the Professor.

"This little document, gentlemen, is a certificate from the register's office at Denver, stating that the Lost Claim, which lies just within this cave here, is the property of Herman von Zepplin. Had you examined this neighborhood more closely you would have found my claim stakes driven, as required by law. With the certificate is a report on the assay of the samples of ore I sent them, showing that, while the mine is a valuable property, it does not contain such untold wealth as generally has been believed. However, it may give these boys a few thousands apiece."

"The Lost Claim! Is it possible?" breathed the boys.

"Yes, Ben Tackers will tell you I am not mistaken. He has known this all along. I had the mine registered in my own name as this was the quickest way to secure it. However, Tad Butler is the rightful owner. Immediately upon our arrival at Denver, I shall take legal measures to transfer the property to him," announced the Professor. Tad slowly shook his head. "It's not mine alone," he answered, gazing at his companions, all of whom, now, were flushed with suppressed excitement. "The Lost Claim belongs to the Pony Rider Boys Club, of which Professor Zepplin is now a member and therefore entitled to share equally with us. Are you willing, fellows?"

"Yes!" they shouted, following it with three cheers and a tiger for Professor Herman von Zepplin.

"As for my share in the claim, Professor, I would prefer that you made it over to my mother," said Tad, with a glad smile. "That is, if no one in the club objects," he added.

"Well, I guess not," replied Ned, with strong emphasis.

Later in the day, the sheriff and his party set out for Eagle Pass with the prisoners. Each member of the gang was sentenced to a term in prison because of the attack on the Pony Rider Boys.

That same day the boys began their preparations for leaving the mountains. At Denver, where they arrived within a week, they effected a sale of the Lost Claim, with the permission of their parents, most of whom came on to fulfill the necessary legal requirements, and when the transfer of the mine had been made, the Pony Rider Boys were twenty-five thousand dollars richer, giving them exactly five thousand dollars apiece. Tad's share was promptly turned over to his mother. Though he did not know it, the money was deposited to his credit in Mr. Perkins's bank.

The exciting experiences of the Pony Rider Boys were not yet at an end. The boys will be heard from again in another volume under the title: "THE PONY RIDER BOYS IN TEXAS; Or, The Veiled Riddle of the Plains." In this forthcoming volume the narrative of how the boys learned to become young plainsmen, and the stirring account of their experiences in the great cattle drive, will be found full of fascination and in every detail true to the strenuous out-door life described.

# Choose from Thousands of 1stWorldLibrary Classics By

Ada Leverson
Adolphus William Ward
Aesop
Agatha Christie
Alexander Aaronsohn
Alexander Kielland
Alexandre Dumas
Alfred Gatty
Alfred Ollivant
Alice Duer Miller
Alice Turner Curtis
Alice Dunbar
Ambrose Bierce
Amelia E. Barr
Andrew Lang
Andrew McFarland Davis
Andy Adams
Anna Sewell
Annie Besant
Annie Hamilton Donnell
Annie Payson Call
Annonaymous
Anton Chekhov
Arnold Bennett
Arthur Conan Doyle
Arthur M. Winfield
Arthur Ransome
Atticus
B.H. Baden-Powell
B. M. Bower
Baroness Emmuska Orczy
Baroness Orczy
Basil King
Bayard Taylor
Ben Macomber
Bertha Muzzy Bower
Bjornstjerne Bjornson
Booth Tarkington
Boyd Cable
Bram Stoker
C. Collodi
C. E. Orr
C. M. Ingleby
Carolyn Wells
Catherine Parr Traill
Charles A. Eastman
Charles Dickens
Charles Dudley Warner
Charles Farrar Browne

Charles Ives
Charles Kingsley
Charles Klein
Charles Lathrop Pack
Charles Whibley
Charles Willing Beale
Charlotte M. Braeme
Charlotte M. Yonge
Charlotte Perkins Stetson
Clair W. Hayes
Clarence Day Jr.
Clarence E. Mulford
Clemence Housman
Confucius
Cornelis DeWitt Wilcox
Cyril Burleigh
D. H. Lawrence
Daniel Defoe
David Garnett
Don Carlos Janes
Donald Keyhoe
Dorothy Kilner
Dougan Clark
Douglas Fairbanks
E. Nesbit
E.P.Roe
E. Phillips Oppenheim
Edgar Rice Burroughs
Edith Van Dyne
Edith Wharton
Edward J. O'Biren
Edward S. Ellis
Edwin L. Arnold
Eleanor Atkins
Eliot Gregory
Elizabeth Gaskell
Elizabeth McCracken
Elizabeth Von Arnim
Ellem Key
Emerson Hough
Emily Dickinson
Enid Bagnold
Enilor Macartney Lane
Erasmus W. Jones
Ernie Howard Pie
Ethel Turner
Ethel Watts Mumford
Eugenie Foa
Eugene Wood

Evelyn Everett-green
Everard Cotes
F. H. Cheley
F. J. Cross
Federick Austin Ogg
Ferdinand Ossendowski
Francis Bacon
Francis Darwin
Frances Hodgson Burnett
Frances Parkinson Keyes
Frank Gee Patchin
Frank Harris
Frank Jewett Mather
Frank L. Packard
Frank V. Webster
Frederic Stewart Isham
Frederick Trevor Hill
Frederick Winslow Taylor
Friedrich Kerst
Friedrich Nietzsche
Fyodor Dostoyevsky
G.A. Henty
G.K. Chesterton
Gabrielle E. Jackson
Garrett P. Serviss
Gaston Leroux
George Ade
Geroge Bernard Shaw
George Durston
George Ebers
George Eliot
George MacDonald
George Meredith
George Orwell
George Tucker
George W. Cable
George Wharton James
Gertrude Atherton
Grace E. King
Grace Gallatin
Grant Allen
Guillermo A. Sherwell
Gulielma Zollinger
Gustav Flaubert
H. A. Cody
H. B. Irving
H.C. Bailey
H. G. Wells
H. H. Munro

H. Irving Hancock
H. Rider Haggard
H. W. C. Davis
Hamilton Wright Mabie
Hans Christian Andersen
Harold Avery
Harold McGrath
Harriet Beecher Stowe
Harry Houidini
Helent Hunt Jackson
Helen Nicolay
Hendrik Conscience
Hendy David Thoreau
Henri Barbusse
Henrik Ibsen
Henry Adams
Henry Ford
Henry Frost
Henry James
Henry Jones Ford
Henry Seton Merriman
Henry W Longfellow
Herbert A. Giles
Herbert N. Casson
Herman Hesse
Homer
Honore De Balzac
Horace Walpole
Horatio Alger Jr.
Howard Pyle
Howard R. Garis
Hugh Lofting
Hugh Walpole
Humphry Ward
Ian Maclaren
Inez Haynes Gillmore
Irving Bacheller
Israel Abrahams
Ivan Turgenev
J.G.Austin
J. Henri Fabre
J. M. Barrie
J. Macdonald Oxley
J. S. Fletcher
J. S. Knowles
J. Storer Clouston
Jack London
Jacob Abbott
James Allen
James Andrews
James Baldwin

James DeMille
James Joyce
James Lane Allen
James Lane Allen
James Oliver Curwood
James Oppenheim
James Otis
James R. Driscoll
Jane Austen
Jens Peter Jacobsen
Jerome K. Jerome
John Burroughs
John Cournos
John F. Kennedy
John Gay
John Glasworthy
John Habberton
John Joy Bell
John Kendrick Bangs
John Milton
John Philip Sousa
Jonas Lauritz Idemil Lie
Jonathan Swift
Joseph A. Altsheler
Joseph Carey
Joseph Conrad
Joseph E. Badger Jr
Joseph Hergesheimer
Joseph Jacobs
Julian Hawthrone
Julies Vernes
Justin Huntly McCarthy
Kakuzo Okakura
Kenneth Grahame
Kenneth McGaffey
Kate Langley Bosher
Kate Langley Bosher
Katherine Cecil Thurston
Katherine Stokes
L. A. Abbot
L. T. Meade
L. Frank Baum
Latta Griswold
Laura Lee Hope
Laurence Housman
Leo Tolstoy
Leonid Andreyev
Lewis Carroll
Lilian Bell
Lloyd Osbourne
Louis Tracy

Louisa May Alcott
Lucy Fitch Perkins
Lucy Maud Montgomery
Lydia Miller Middleton
Lyndon Orr
M. Corvus
M. H. Adams
Margaret E. Sangster
Margaret Vandercook
Margret Penrose
Maria Edgeworth
Maria Thompson Daviess
Mariano Azuela
Marion Polk Angellotti
Mark Overton
Mark Twain
Mary Austin
Mary Catherine Crowley
Mary Cole
Mary Hastings Bradley
Mary Roberts Rinehart
Mary Rowlandson
M. Wollstonecraft Shelley
Maud Lindsay
Max Beerbohm
Myra Kelly
Nathaniel Hawthrone
Nicolo Machiavelli
O. F. Walton
Oscar Wilde
Owen Johnson
P.G. Wodehouse
Paul and Mabel Thorne
Paul G. Tomlinson
Paul Severing
Percy Brebner
Peter B. Kyne
Plato
R. Derby Holmes
R. L. Stevenson
R. S. Ball
Rabindranath Tagore
Rahul Alvares
Ralph Henry Barbour
Ralph Waldo Emmerson
Rene Descartes
Rex Beach
Rex E. Beach
Richard Harding Davis
Richard Jefferies
Richard Le Gallienne

Robert Barr
Robert Frost
Robert Gordon Anderson
Robert L. Drake
Robert Lansing
Robert Lynd
Robert Michael Ballantyne
Robert W. Chambers
Rosa Nouchette Carey
Rudyard Kipling
Samuel B. Allison
Samuel Hopkins Adams
Sarah Bernhardt
Selma Lagerlof
Sherwood Anderson
Sigmund Freud
Standish O'Grady
Stanley Weyman
Stella Benson
Stephen Crane
Stewart Edward White
Stijn Streuvels
Swami Abhedananda

Swami Parmananda
T. S. Ackland
T. S. Arthur
The Princess Der Ling
Thomas A. Janvier
Thomas A Kempis
Thomas Anderton
Thomas Bailey Aldrich
Thomas Bulfinch
Thomas De Quincey
Thomas H. Huxley
Thomas Hardy
Thomas More
Thornton W. Burgess
U. S. Grant
Valentine Williams
Various Authors
Victor Appleton
Virginia Woolf
Walter Camp
Walter Scott
Washington Irving
Wilbur Lawton

Wilkie Collins
Willa Cather
Willard F. Baker
William Dean Howells
William le Queux
W. Makepeace Thackeray
William W. Walter
Winston Churchill
Yei Theodora Ozaki
Yogi Ramacharaka
Young E. Allison
Zane Grey